DENIM &

DIAMONDS

Elle Robb

Enjoy!
Elle Robb
2/24/06

This is a work of fiction. Names, characters, places and incidents either are the product of the author's imagination or are used fictitiously, and any resemblance to actual persons, living or dead, business establishments, events, or locales is entirely coincidental.

Copyright © 2006 by Lori Robinett

All rights reserved. This book, or parts thereof,

may not be produced in any form without

permission

ISBN 1-4116-7789-7

Printed in the United States of America

Book design by Lori Robinett

Cover photography by Lori and JR Robinett

To JR and Katelyn *– thank you for putting up with the constant presence of the laptop . . . you are my inspiration and reason for being.*

And to Lynn *– thank you for being supportive, and for being the vent I turn to when the pressure cooker threatens to blow.*

Introduction

Some of you may be familiar with National Novel Writing Month. It is the brainchild of Chris Baty, and takes place during November of each year. I was introduced to NaNoWriMo during 2003, and participated for the first time in '04. The goal of NaNoWriMo is to write 50,000 words in one month. It starts at 12:01 a.m. on November 1, and ends at midnight on November 30. If you take the challenge and participate in forums, you may well find yourself hooked up with a local group, attending Write-Ins and, best of all, that TGIO (Thank God It's Over!) party at the beginning of December!

The comment that I get from many people is "Really, you wrote a novel in a month?" and the next words, unspoken, are clear in their faces, "But it must be crap, huh?" That's the reason this book is being published – I wrote Denim & Diamonds during NaNoWriMo 2004. I have used spell check, and I did edit it for mistakes, though I tried to remain true to the story that was written during that challenge – to hopefully inspire others to participate in future NaNoWriMo challenges. If you have ever said, "Someday, I will write a novel" – read this book and take it as a challenge. If I did it, you can do it!

Elle

Denim & Diamonds

CHAPTER ONE

Beth peered nervously through the driving sheets of rain, slowing down even more. The windshield wipers swished, but weren't keeping up with the torrent. She flipped the switch to high and the wipers flip-flipped frantically, but she still couldn't see any better. The crackle of the radio irritated her already jangled nerves. She frowned and glanced down just for a second to flip the radio off, but when she looked up there was a flash of brown and white fur in her headlights. She swerved, and slammed her right foot down on the brakes. The car skidded wildly on the wet blacktop. She spun the steering wheel, desperately trying to correct the skid. The car skidded right, then left, then plowed through the ditch. Her head snapped forward, striking the steering wheel. The seatbelt cut painfully into her stomach and chest.

It was all over in a split-second. She slumped in her seat, her breath ragged and painful. She blinked slowly. The windshield wipers still flip-flopped, and the rain thumped angrily against the roof of her Camry. She took a couple of deep breaths, and ran through a mental inventory of her limbs. Everything seemed to be attached and was still working. Gingerly, she touched her forehead and was glad the gash seemed to be small, and not bleeding badly. Her car was still running. That was good. No airbag. That was bad. She glanced back at the road. No Bambi corpse. That was good. She carefully put the gearshift in reverse and pressed gently on the gas. The wheels spun in the mud and grass, but there was no traction. That was bad. And things were starting to tilt, and the darkness seemed to be closing in. That was really bad . . .

Headlights swept over her car and she looked over her shoulder just in time to see a jacked-up truck pull over on the shoulder behind her. She wondered for a moment if this was good or bad. Good if he was the hero-type. Bad if he was the ax murderer type. The way her luck was running, it could go either way. She felt herself start to drift off.

The knock on her window startled her. For a moment there, she had thought she was dreaming. She looked out and saw the perfect man. She was sure she had seen him in a cigarette ad once upon a time. But then again, she vaguely seemed to remember that he had died.

"Ma'am! Ma'am! Are you okay?" The cowboy shouted over a clap of thunder.

She nodded slowly, admiring his strong, angular face and dark, brooding eyes. She sighed when she realized he was wearing a black cowboy hat, and a leather duster. Perfect. The door swung open and suddenly the cowboy was only inches away. She smiled in what she hoped was seductive way, and brushed a stray tendril of hair out of her face.

"Hi." Her voice sounded hollow.

"Hi, yourself. Are you sure you're okay?" His voice was deep and warm, a nice contrast to the cold, blowing rain. Frown lines creased his tanned forehead. She didn't know cowboys were still around, rescuing damsels in distress. A giggle escaped at the thought that she was a damsel in distress.

"I had an accident," she answered.

"I see that. What happened?" the cowboy asked.

His eyes were roaming over her. Maybe checking her out, maybe looking for blood. She shrugged.

"An animal ran in front of me and I swerved. I guess I'm in a ditch. My car's stuck." Beth smiled and took

Denim & Diamonds

a shaky breath. He didn't smell at all like cigarettes. He smelled good. It sort of reminded her of fresh grass.

"Don't you know you should never swerve to miss an animal? It's dangerous." He reached in and took her gently by the arm, to help her out of the car. She thought that being so close to him was pretty dangerous, too. Her experience with men was limited to city types, mostly accountants and lawyers. No cowboys that she could recall.

He helped her up to his truck, both of them slipping and sliding up the rain-slicked grass, the rain relentless in its pursuit of them, and put her in on the passenger side. She watched as he slipped back down the bank and walked around her car, leaning down a couple of times to take a closer look at the damage. It was hard to see his ass because of the long duster, but she was pretty sure it was nice. The water pouring down the glass distorted everything, and it all seemed like a dream. She sighed and let her head fall back against the rough cloth of the seat. Her head was starting to throb, and she was so, so tired. She didn't hear him open the door, and didn't feel the truck start to move.

Beau slowed when he spotted the black and white Domino Ranch sign swinging in the wind, marking the entrance to the ranch. He swung into the long, curved driveway. The rain was still coming down so hard, he could barely see. The only way he stayed on the drive was by watching the white fencing that lined the drive. He glanced over at the woman he had rescued. She must have had quite a bump to the head, but at least it seemed to have stopped bleeding. He still wasn't sure he'd done the right thing by bringing her to the ranch. He maybe should've just taken her straight to the hospital in Moscow. Or called for an ambulance. Charlotte would probably give him a dressing down for moving her.

He parked in his usual spot, just to the right of the steps of the big house. He was glad to see Charlotte's black Suburban there. She'd know what to do. She was good with people. He wasn't. He beeped his horn several times and the massive front door opened. Charlotte's short, stout figure was outlined in the doorway for a moment as she peered out, probably trying to figure out why he was raising such a racket on a dark, rainy night. Beau jumped out of the Chevy and ran around to the passenger side.

"Charlotte! This woman had an accident out on the blacktop!" he shouted as he pulled the still-limp redhead from the truck. He picked her up like she was nothing and quickly strode up the wide steps and into the house. He sat her down on the bench under the coat rack, and he and Charlotte leaned over the stranger, checking her for injuries. Charlotte pulled a handkerchief from her pocket and dabbed gently at the gash on the young woman's forehead. Suddenly, Charlotte gasped and grabbed Beau's arm.

"Dear Lord, boy! Do you know who this is? This is Beth Pickard!"

"Oh?" Beau looked at the woman he'd rescued. Her red curls were escaping from the loose ponytail, and wet tendrils stuck to her round face. There were freckles sprinkled across her nose and cheeks. Her pink tongue poked out and she licked her full lips slowly. This certainly wasn't the prissy ice queen he had been expecting. For one thing, she looked younger than he expected a high-powered city accountant to be. For another, this woman seemed, well, warm. Soft. And she had a wonderful smile, even though she had looked a little dizzy when she was smiling at him. She had seemed so sweet. Then again, she had just whacked her head in a car wreck. Put her in a power suit and tame that hair in a tight bun and she might be one tough customer.

"Beau! Snap out of it! Go get some towels. We've got to get her dried off." Charlotte started mumbling to herself. Something about concussions and screwing up first impressions. Beau escaped to find towels.

When Beau returned, the young woman was smiling that wonderful smile again, only this time it was directed at Charlotte. She shrugged self-consciously, ". . . so, I

Denim & Diamonds

swerved. Not the best response given the situation, I know, but I just reacted." Beth shook her head slowly, "It would just kill me to hurt an animal, though."

"I'm the same way," Charlotte confessed. "I even cry if I hit a squirrel or a 'coon."

The woman looked around and blinked, trying to get her bearings. "I don't mean to be rude, but where am I and how did I get here?"

"You're at Domino Ranch, and I brought you here." Beau handed a big, thirsty towel to the woman, careful not to let their fingers touch, and laid another on the bench next to her. "You had an accident and I stopped to help. You were pretty shook up, so I brought you here for Charlotte's expert nursing advice."

Beth nodded slowly, blotting her hair with the towel. "I'm glad you stopped."

Beau shrugged, "That's what folks out here do. I'm just glad I happened to be driving by. Wouldn't have been out, 'cept I ran into town to get some antibiotics from the vet for a mare that just lost her foal."

She frowned and said, "A minute ago, um, did you say Domino Ranch?"

He nodded, but Charlotte answered.

"Yes, Mr. Cooper called ahead and told us to expect you tonight. It was getting late enough, I actually thought you might have decided to spend the night in Moscow before coming on out to the ranch."

Beau cleared his throat, "I'm sorry I didn't recognize you sooner, Miss Pickard."

"Please, call me Beth." She looked from the older woman to the cowboy. She blushed as she remembered thinking he was the Marlboro man. Hopefully, she hadn't voiced those particular thoughts. "You have me at a disadvantage. You both know me, but . . . "

Beau quickly introduced himself as the ranch foreman, and then excused himself after he was sure the accident victim he'd saved wasn't going to keel over and didn't need a ride to the hospital.

Beth looked around the large living room, which was dominated by a large stone fireplace. Above the mantle hung a huge portrait of her father kneeling on one leg with his arm around a black and white dog. A chandelier made from antlers hung from rough-hewn beams. The exposed log walls added to the rustic feel of the room. The furniture was mostly brown leather. Definitely masculine, and not a touch of feminine anywhere, she noted. She looked down at the hardwood floors and realized that rain water was pooling at her feet.

She said softly, "I'm sorry, I seem to be getting everything wet."

The older woman helped Beth to her feet and led her through the living room and the arched doorway on the left. "Quite all right, quite all right. Let's go find you some dry clothes and a warm bed. Oh! And I guess you'll want to be knowin' who I am. I'm Charlotte. Don't have a title. We're pretty informal around here. I just sort of take care of everything around the houses. I cook, I clean. Whatever needs to be done, I do it."

"I see. You must have known my father well, then." Beth said it as a statement, but Charlotte took it as a question.

"I did, and I wish to extend my deepest sympathies to you. Your father was a wonderful man, and he will be – I take that back – he *is* missed deeply. I apologize for not extending my sympathies to you at the funeral. You just seemed so overwhelmed, I didn't think you needed to be bothered with an old woman like me," Charlotte said as she stopped in the third doorway on their left.

"You came to the funeral?" Beth asked, wondering what else she had missed that day. It had been such a blur. Such a shock. The whole thing had been so strange. She hadn't seen her father in, goodness, probably three or four years, and hadn't talked to him on the phone since he called her on her birthday last spring.

"Of course, Beau and I both did. Your father was like family," Charlotte motioned for Beth to enter the room

Denim & Diamonds

first. "I know you've had a long day, so I won't keep you. I think you'll find everything here that you'll need. Just look through the drawers, and the closet. Towels are in the linen closet. Extra things like toothpaste and shampoo are under the sink."

"I'm sure I'll be fine." Beth answered, as she took in her surroundings. This room was more of a suite, with a sitting area by the bay window. It was larger than most hotel rooms she had stayed in, and was much larger than her own bedroom in her condo in Overland Park. Her gaze settled on the beautiful wrought iron canopy bed that dominated the room.

"Breakfast is at 7. Hope you like bacon, eggs and flapjacks," Charlotte said as she turned to leave.

"I don't usually eat breakfast," Beth said.

"You may want to eat a big breakfast while you're here. Beau will look after your car for you in the morning, but then I'm sure he'll want to show you around the ranch. You'll be needin' your strength to keep up with him!" Charlotte frowned as her gaze settled on the discolored egg rising on Beth's forehead, "That is, if you feel up to it."

"I'm sure I'll be fine," She felt a blush creep up her cheeks as she thought of spending a day with the cowboy. Her heart raced at the thought, "So, Beau is the ranch manager?"

"Yes. He is – was – pretty much your father's right hand man."

"Oh," Beth said, not sure what else to say. She had a sudden mental image of the Duke boys sliding over the hood of the General Lee. A different image from the cowboy, but still, pretty sexy. She gave her head a little shake. That bump to her head must have been worse than she thought. Either that, or the whole episode with her fiance – ex-fiance, she reminded herself sternly – had gotten to her more than she wanted to admit.

Charlotte said kindly, "Now you just holler if you need anything, I am in the room just kitty-cornered across the hallway."

7

Elle Robb

Finally alone, Beth stared at the closed door for nearly a full minute, just trying to take it all in and convince herself that this was real. She was honestly standing in the – correction, *a* – guest bedroom at her father's ranch. She turned to take a closer look at the room. The furniture was beautiful, an eclectic mix of antique and new. Her favorite part was the tall canopy bed, covered with a double-wedding ring quilt and several pillows of different sizes, shapes and all different shades of pink. Even the dust ruffle and the tulle wound around the canopy frame was pink.

She caught herself smiling as she realized that there was no way her father had decorated this room. Most likely, he'd never even been in here if the living room was any indication of his decorating tastes. Her smile faded as she wondered if this room had been set up for his mistresses. Though her mother had tried to protect her from the rumors, she had always heard that her father was quite the playboy. Ever since her parents had divorced when she was ten, her mother had told her that her father was too busy with his various women to spend time with his daughter.

She shook the mental image from her head and began searching through chest of drawers, surprised to finds clothes in several styles, sizes and colors. She settled on a pair of gray sweats and a gray T-shirt, glad to be out of her wet clothes. At least the rain hadn't soaked through to her panties, for which she was very thankful. After she got ready for bed in the equally feminine bathroom, she set the old-fashioned alarm clock on the nightstand. The pale pink flannel sheets were wonderful, soft and comforting as she slipped into bed, and drifted off to dream of cowboys hood-sliding across the General Lee.

CHAPTER TWO

Beth woke with a start, and it took her a moment to realize that someone was knocking on her door. Just as she sat up, the wooden door opened with a slight creak and Charlotte poked her head in.

"Breakfast is ready," Charlotte said.

"Thanks, but I don't usually eat breakfast. I think I'd like to get my bags from my car. And I need to do something about my car. I just can't be without my car. And I need to figure out what I'm doing here." Beth sighed heavily, "I'm sorry. You've been very nice to me. I know I was a little goofy last night. I'm used to being more in control. I've really got to get some things taken care of."

Charlotte nodded slowly and seemed to consider the options. "Fair enough. I can call Cletus up at the station and have him tow your car to his shop and take a look at it. And I'll take you to town after I finish cleaning up from breakfast, so you can get your bags. How does that sound?"

"That'll work," Beth replied. She swung her feet off the bed, and wiggled her toes in the sheepskin rug. She thought for a moment and asked, "This Cletus – is he reputable?"

"Don't think I've ever heard the term 'reputable' connected to that boy, but if you're asking me if he'll do you right, he most certainly will. He grew up in these parts and knows better than to try to pull something over on a Pickard!"

"Then I would appreciate it if you would call him," Beth said as she reached for the robe draped over the foot of the bed. "I'm going to freshen up and then I'll be down."

Once she was alone, she looked through the big walk-in closet and found a pair of jeans that looked like they would fit, and found a plain teal blue t-shirt that she thought would work. It was better than most of the t-shirts that filled the closet, emblazoned with various local feed store names and farm supply store logos. She couldn't imagine why anyone would go to the trouble of having a cedar-lined closet, and then fill it with garbage like that.

Once she was satisfied with her choice of clothing, she decided a nice, long shower would help her feel better. Her head still throbbed and she could feel the egg rising on her forehead. She let the hot water run over her body, and lathered up with the peach-scented shower gel that she found in one of the drawers. It felt so good, but she knew she had to get out and face the day. The Egyptian cotton towel was top drawer, and she was surprised to see that all of the towels and linens were monogrammed with a "P". And the sheets had definitely been a very high thread count. Her father had never seemed the type to pay attention to that sort of thing. She couldn't help but wonder who the woman was – though the main living area of the house had been very masculine, this room had definitely felt a woman's touch. It was a little disconcerting to think about her father's affairs.

She explored the cabinets and was surprised to find a wide variety of makeup and toiletries. After she had made use of them, and was fairly satisfied that she was presentable, she decided she could put it off no longer. She headed out of her room, and made her way to the kitchen.

The sounds told her Charlotte was cleaning up before she turned the corner. She smiled as she recognized the theme to "Green Acres". Her eyes widened when she saw how big the kitchen table was – it would have easily

Denim & Diamonds

sat at least a dozen people. There was a beautiful crocheted lace doily runner, and the centerpiece was a large stoneware crock filled with cut flowers.

"Wow!" she exclaimed, "I don't think I've ever seen a kitchen table that big before!"

"And we make good use of it, too. Your father was fond of having meals here. They were always big affairs – lots of good food and good company, he used to say." Charlotte wiped off her hands on the dish towel and untied her apron. "Can I talk you into some breakfast now, child?"

"No, thank you. Did you call the mechanic about my car?"

"I did. Said he'd already seen it and towed it to town."

"I see," Beth was irritated that someone would tow her car without checking to make sure she wanted it towed, but she chose to keep her thoughts to herself for the moment, "Did he say how bad it was?"

"No," said Charlotte as she flipped the coffee maker off. "Thought you'd want to discuss that with him yourself. You ready for me to run you to town now?"

On the way to town, Beth watched the sides of the winding blacktop, curious to see where she had wrecked. Sure enough, just a short ways down the road, there was a spot where the grass had been smashed down and ruts marked where her car had been. A small sapling hadn't survived the wreck, and was leaning awkwardly with a large gash in its trunk. Just about three feet in front of the tire marks, there was a woven wire fence stretched tightly between thick wooden posts.

"That must be where I wrecked last night."

"Looks that way. I'd say you were lucky. Been goin' a little faster and you'd a gone right through that fence."

"That would have been bad." Beth said, turning back to look at the spot.

"You bet it would have. That's the pasture where your daddy's polled Hereford bull is. He'd plow you over in the blink of an eye," Charlotte said, "And Beau would have had your tail if he'd had to go round that bull up!"

The two chatted for the remaining twenty minutes or so, mostly about safe topics like the weather. Charlotte shared a few stories, but Beth felt a little odd that the man described seemed so much nicer and friendlier than the cold, hard father-figure she had known. They topped a hill and the little town of Moscow was spread out before them. The first thing Beth noticed was the three church spires that dotted the "skyline". As Charlotte drove her Suburban down Main Street, Beth counted three taverns, two antique stores and a café. Several storefronts were obviously empty. The only new building in town appeared to be the bank, which proudly proclaimed, "Free Cooler with New Account" on a neon yellow banner hanging on the front of the building. She couldn't help but raise her eyebrows when she saw the service station. There was one gas pump, and it looked like it had been there since the 1930's. There was a hand-painted sign hanging above the one service bay that said simply "Mechanic", except "ech" was nearly worn away, so it looked like, "M   anic". Her maroon Toyota was the only car in the lot. She turned and looked back down Main Street, and realized that there was not another car on the street. There appeared to be a law that everyone in Moscow was required to drive a truck. Preferably four-wheel drive. And rusty. Charlotte beeped the horn twice and put the Suburban in Park. When they got out, Beth noticed that the keys were left dangling from the ignition switch. She started to say something and then stopped herself. Better to watch, listen and learn.

A grease-covered man who appeared to be in his late fifties came out of the service bay, wiping his hands on a red rag. "Good mornin', Miss Charlotte."

"Good morning, Cletus." Charlotte motioned towards Beth, "This is Beth Pickard, Mr. Pickard's daughter. It's her car that you towed this morning."

Cletus nodded at Beth, "Pleased to meet ya, Miss Pickard."

Denim & Diamonds

"Please, call me Beth. Thank you for towing my car. It doesn't look too bad, but it does look like it needs some work."

"Yes, ma'am, but not much. Just put a hole in the oil pan, and your bumper'll have to be replaced." Cletus scratched his head, leaving a greasy shock of hair sticking straight up. "Have to order the bumper. Should be done in, oh, two weeks. Mebbe three."

Beth raised her eyebrows, "Two or three weeks? Why so long?"

"Oh, I just don't want to promise somethin' I cain't deliver, Miss Pickard. And Frank Holloway is puttin' up a new barn that I told him I'd help with. I done promised him, so I gotta do that first." Cletus smiled, his two missing teeth making him look like a jack o' lantern.

"You can drive my Suburban anytime you need to," Charlotte said.

Beth hated the idea of being dependent on someone else, but after looking up and down Main Street again, she decided she really didn't have much of an option. She sighed and said, "I guess that'll work. Can you give me an estimate before you start the work?"

"Well," Cletus said, drawing the word out, "It'll be hard to know how much 'til I get in there. Want me to give you a call when I got it tore up?"

She looked at Charlotte, who was smiling her encouragement. She gave up, "Just fix it, please. And call me as soon as it's done?"

Charlotte stepped in and took over, explaining that Beth would be staying out at the ranch. Cletus volunteered to drive the car out to the ranch once the work was done, and the arrangements were complete. Cletus offered to get her bags for her out of the Camry but, after she considered the probability that he would end up leaving quite a big of grease on her luggage, she chose to do it herself. After her bags had been transferred to the Suburban, the two women hopped in and headed for the ranch. As they drove, Charlotte pointed out various things that she thought would

13

be of interest to a newcomer. Nearly every house they passed had some connection to Domino Ranch, and it became apparent that Jonathan Pickard had been a popular figure in this little town. She couldn't help but wonder if that was what had drawn him to this area – the whole big fish in a small pond theory. The man she knew loved power, and loved wielding it. But these stories indicated a different type of person.

After they returned to the ranch and Beth had gotten the luggage into her room, she dug through her briefcase for the document that had dominated her thoughts for the past two weeks. Once she had it in her hands, she wanted to read it again. And she knew exactly where she wanted to be when she read it. She headed down the hall for her father's library, which she had noticed that morning.

She stood in the doorway for a moment, took a deep breath and then moved to the big oak desk that dominated the room. She sat carefully in the leather chair. She placed the document squarely in front of her and closed her eyes for a moment. The faint scent of leather and fine cigars and old books evoked memories of her father. She had never realized before that she associated those smells with her father. She quickly wiped her eyes, before a tear could fall. She blinked rapidly, took a deep breath and looked around the room.

The old-style globe to her right was fascinating. It was the type of thing that made you want to dream of destinations unknown. She ran her fingers over the surface, feeling the bump of the mountains and the smoothness of the vast oceans. She reached the equator and felt a seam. She flipped the globe open, and found a half empty bottle of Chivas and two glasses. Now, this was the father that she knew. She closed the globe, but made a mental note that this was the place to come if things got a little too tense.

The walls were lined with shelves, full of books. Most were beautiful, old, leather-bound volumes. She suspected that many of the books had been chosen purely for their value, because the only thing she could remember

Denim & Diamonds

her father reading was the Wall Street Journal. The two large windows allowed in lots of light, which contrasted nicely with the dark wood that lined the room. Each window had a simple pedestal in front of it, with a Remington statue on each one. She was a little surprised they weren't covered with glass. Then she wondered if they were insured.

OK, enough procrastination, she thought, and turned her attention back to the document in front of her. With it, her father had taken his last stab at controlling her life. Her lips moved as she read.

"I, Jonathan Richard Pickard, of Cardwell County, Kansas, do hereby devise and bequeath my real estate in Cardwell County, Kansas, commonly known as Domino Ranch, to my daughter, Beth Catherine Pickard, to be held in trust for one year. It is my intention and desire that my daughter, Beth Catherine Pickard, live on the ranch and manage the ranch. My said daughter must keep all employees that were employed by Domino Ranch on the day of my death, except and unless she has the written consent of my Trustee. On the one year anniversary of my death, my Trustee of this residence trust shall determine whether or not my said daughter has been able to manage the Domino Ranch in a profitable and successful manner. In the event she is able to manage the Domino Ranch in a profitable and successful manner, in the sole and absolute discretion of my Trustee,

```
then said Domino Ranch will be
given to my said daughter
outright, though it is my hope and
desire that my said daughter will
continue to own and operate the
Domino Ranch as I would have if I
had survived. In the event my said
daughter shall fail or refuse to
live on the real estate, then the
real estate commonly known as
Domino Ranch shall be distributed
to Charlotte Ann Jennings and  . .
. "
```

So, there it was. She was here. Apparently, her father could still control her life. She felt like she was 10 again, and he was making her take dance classes and wear one of those horrible costumes. She made a face at the paper. "Bastard!"

"I'm sorry?" Charlotte asked from the doorway.

Beth looked up, her face flushed with embarrassment. "Nothing. Um, I was just thinking."

Charlotte looked around the room fondly, "This was your father's favorite room. He was in here nearly every evening. Do you enjoy Louis L'Amour books, too?"

"My father read Louis L'Amour?" Beth asked, her voice full of disbelief.

Charlotte came into the room and ran her hands over the back of one of the wingbacked chairs facing the fireplace. "He'd sit right here, with the fire going, and read for hours."

"I see," Beth said, not really seeing at all. That just didn't mesh with the stern, no-nonsense man that occasionally visited her in the City. And Charlotte had an almost dreamy look in her hazel eyes. Beth cleared her throat, "Anyway, I guess I need to have a meeting with all the employees. Can you let everyone know to meet me right before dinner, this afternoon?"

Denim & Diamonds

"I, I guess I can do that." Charlotte said, her eyebrows raised.

"Good," Beth said, feeling better now that she had taken some action, "Is there a place we can meet?"

"The kitchen?" Charlotte shrugged.

"The kitchen will be fine. I'll see you there at 5." Beth turned her attention back to her father's will. Charlotte stood awkwardly for a moment, and then slipped from the room without another word.

At 5 sharp, Charlotte had everyone assembled in the kitchen, as instructed. Beth had spent the afternoon in her father's library, making notes and trying to come up with ideas for running a successful, profitable ranch. She loved a challenge, and she loved numbers. This was a challenge she was going to win. She checked her appearance, and her heels clicked smartly on the hardwood floor of the hallway. It always amazed her how much more confident she felt when she changed into what she considered her power uniform.

The voices in the kitchen grew quiet before she entered the room. All eyes turned to see the boss's daughter, who they'd all heard about by this point. She was the picture of professionalism, in a black fitted pantsuit, with a red camisole peeking out of the jacket. Her red curls had been pulled back into a bun to keep them under control. Beau leaned out and looked down at her shoes. It was clear from his expression that he thought heels like that had no place on a ranch.

She started her speech, which she had rehearsed well. She explained that her father had left the ranch to her, with the caveat that it be profitable. In a firm voice, she explained that she would take whatever steps were necessary to make the ranch profitable during the coming year. She ended by promising that no one's job was in danger, and that she would do her best to be a fair and impartial employer. No one spoke until she had finished, and then Beau cleared his throat.

"Miss Pickard, we've all worked for your father a long time. Your father treated us well, and we would do anything for him. If he saw fit to leave the Domino Ranch to you, then we'll do anything for you," he paused and looked around the room, "I think I speak for all of us."

There was a general murmur of agreement. She looked around the room, careful to make eye contact with everyone.

"But it's my understanding," the ranch manager continued, "That you're a city girl. So, we hope you don't go changing things too much around here. No offense intended."

"None taken," she answered quickly, though color brightened her cheeks. She said, " I think that's all I needed for now. My door is always open. Thank you all."

Charlotte took over as Beth click-clicked back down the hallway to her room. As she retreated down the hall, she could hear the sounds of dinner starting. After she changed back into her jeans and t-shirt, she went to join the group for dinner. The conversation stopped when she entered the room, causing her cheeks to brighten again. Beau sat at the head of the table, and Charlotte offered her the foot of the table. With a smile, she declined and sat next to one of the ranch hands, a deeply tanned young man with unruly blonde hair and bright blue eyes. Food was passed, and talk turned to the events of the day. Words like "bits" and "frogs" swirled around her with little meaning, and she found herself looking forward to returning to the privacy of her bedroom. She clenched her fists and smiled politely, determined to make the best of the situation she'd been thrown into.

Denim & Diamonds

<u>**CHAPTER THREE**</u>

Beth awoke to the soft beep-beep of her little travel alarm clock. She shut it off and snuggled back down into the wonderful scent of lavender. She touched her forehead tenderly, wincing as her fingers brushed the big bump that seemed even larger than it had yesterday. Her head was throbbing slightly. She opened her eyes and looked around the room, remembering the events of the day before. She carefully sat up and slid off the bed, the sheepskin rug feeling incredibly warm and comforting to her bare feet. She pulled the lace drapes to the side and saw that the sun was just starting to turn the sky shades of pink, purple and orange. Looked like it was going to be a clear day. She checked the closet and found a sweatshirt and pair of jeans that she thought would fit. Before long, she would need to go shopping. The clothes she had packed weren't quite what she needed out on the ranch.

The sky was lightening quickly and the house was quiet. On impulse, Beth pulled her Keds on and headed down the hallway without freshening up. She'd never seen a sunrise in the country before. Come to think of it, she'd never seen a sunrise at all. Not on purpose or for pleasure, anyway. And no one was up, so she could just let her hair down for a little while and enjoy being out here. It was just so beautiful, and she couldn't help but feel positive about this new venture.

Elle Robb

Once on the front porch, she took a deep breath. The air really was better out here. She heard a meow and looked down to see a calico cat sitting at the bottom of the steps staring at her. She started down the steps to pet the cat, but just as she got to the bottom step, the cat hopped away.

"My goodness, kitty. You've only got three legs!" She said, moving slowly towards the brightly colored cat. The cat meowed, but it was a funny meow, sort of without the "m". She thought that it sounded a lot like the little cat was saying "Ow". Once again, when she drew near, the cat hopped away. This continued several times until the two had gone across the yard and the drive. Then the cat hopped under the white wooden fence and into the pasture. There was a strange attraction to the cat and Beth finally opened the gate, after fiddling with it a moment to figure the latch out. The cat meowed again. She glanced around, but she and the cat seemed to be completely alone. Apparently, no one was up yet. She wondered briefly where the horses and dogs were that her father had spoken so fondly of.

She and the cat continued their journey. The cat headed through the lush grass for a group of trees, and she followed, feeling a bit like Timmy following Lassie. Water was flowing and bubbling just ahead. As she got to the edge of the trees, she realized that a stream ran through the trees. It was such a peaceful setting, and literally looked like something right out of a movie. The calico cat was perched on a rock at the top of a little waterfall, grooming itself carefully. Beth sat down on large, smooth rock at the edge of the stream, and began talking softly to the cat. It was so peaceful with the babbling of the brook, the sun just beginning to shine through the trees . . .

"Damn it! Hey! I need help NOW!" came a shout from behind her. Beau's voice broke the calm of the morning, and she sprang to her feet. The little cat continued to clean its orange and white face, oblivious to the yelling. She took one last look at the cat, decided the cat would be fine on its own, and quickly headed back the way she'd come. Her heart sank when she cleared the trees.

Beau was in the driveway, waving his arms at the two horses trying to head down the drive toward the highway. Another horse was happily grazing on the lush green grass in the front yard. And the gate she had gone through was wide open. Two men came running from the small cabin, and a teenaged girl came running from the barn, halters and leads in both hands. She closed her eyes tightly for a moment and cursed herself for being so stupid as to leave a gate open, then ran towards the gate, hoping to salvage the situation by helping get the horses back in the pasture. Beau spotted her when she was just about to the gate. The anger flashing in his eyes was hard to mistake.

"You!" he yelled, "Get the hell away from that gate! We're trying to get them *in*, not scare them away!"

"Where do you want me?" she asked, trying to keep her voice from cracking.

"Over here!" yelled the girl with the ponytail. She motioned to follow her along the fence. The girl tossed one halter to Beau and handed another to Beth. She held the tangle of leather bunched up, not having any idea which side was up, but she was determined to stay close to the girl, who looked like she knew what she was doing even if she couldn't have been more than 12 or 13. At the very least, Beth thought could hold the halter until someone needed it. The girl was intense, completely focused on the animals in front of her. She moved sideways slowly, her back to the fence. Beth followed suit. The two horses in the driveway were focused on Beau, who was talking to them constantly. The girl held her halter loosely, with the cotton lead thrown over her shoulder. Her steps were sure and confident as she approached the smaller of the two escapees. The brown horse saw her, nodded his head and pawed the ground. Beth was close enough to see the white showing around his eyes, and she was amazed at how muscular the animal was. The girl talked softly to the horse, and approached him slowly. When she got beside him, she gently pulled the halter over his head. Once caught, he stood patiently, waiting to be led.

The other horse was watching everything intently, his ears pricked forward. He seemed calm enough and Beth decided to make her move. She tried to imitate the girl, and began walking toward the animal, talking to him as she went. He let her get right up to him, but she didn't know how to put the halter on. She glanced at the bay the girl was holding, and thought she could manage. It didn't look that hard. She lifted her hands to put the halter over his head, but he ducked his head and spun away from her. Fortunately, Beau was right there. He threw his arm over the horse's neck and had the halter on and buckled in seconds. The cowboy looked at her and let his breath out through flared nostrils, his jaw muscles working furiously.

"You don't ever, *ever* go through a gate and leave it open," he hissed, "Do you understand me?"

"It wasn't on purpose. I didn't know." Tears stung her eyes, and she bit her lower lip to keep it from trembling.

"Well, now you know." Beau tossed over his shoulder as he and the teenager led the horses back to the gate. The other two men already had the horse from the yard back in the pasture and were waiting at the gate to help get the other two horses in. She gathered up every ounce of self esteem she had and forced herself to walk up the drive. The four ranch employees watched her silently from the gate. The stocky, dark-haired man spit tobacco juice on the ground just as she pulled even with them.

"I may have made a mistake, but I am still your boss," she said as she turned to face the four, her own jaw set now. "Make no mistake about that."

Denim & Diamonds

CHAPTER FOUR

Beth hid in her father's library for the next couple of hours, jotting notes, sketching plans for the ranch, and licking her wounded pride. She wasn't used to failure, and she absolutely hated making mistakes. Particularly mistakes that were as spectacularly stupid as leaving the gate to the horse pasture open. The worst part was that her employees had a front row seat for her screw up. It was hard enough to deal with people in general, much less people who didn't think you were competent.

She sighed. That was why she liked being an accountant. She sat in her neat, organized office and dealt with numbers all day. With numbers, you could check your work and know it was right. And numbers forgave you. You make a mistake, you fix it. No grudges, no doubts. And worst of all, Beau had looked at her as if she were the stupidest person on the face of the earth. The contempt in his eyes had cut her to the core. She jumped when Charlotte knocked softly on the door.

"Come in," she said. Before she looked up from her sketches, she smelled the beef stew and fresh sourdough bread that Charlotte had so thoughtfully brought to her. Charlotte sat the serving tray on the desk and motioned toward the leather guest chair that faced the desk.

"Mind if I sit?" Charlotte asked, one eyebrow raised.

"Please do. And thank you. I was starting to get a little hungry."

"Go ahead and eat, child. I'll stay and talk, if you don't mind." Charlotte pushed the tray across the desk. Her hands were strong and tanned, and her short nails were painted with clear polish. Beth took the offered food and was not surprised to find that it was delicious. The stew had a kick to it, and it was full of potatoes, which were her favorite vegetable. She closed her eyes and savored the stew.

It had been so long since she'd had anything close to home cooked food. Much, much better than the Lean Cuisines or Pizza Rolls that were such a staple of her diet. Living alone in a condo and working 60 hour weeks wasn't exactly conducive to homecooked meals. Even when she'd lived at home with her mother, most meals had been quick, ready-to-eat meals or they'd gone out. Then she and Bob had moved in together, but they both worked such long hours, they usually had take-out.

Charlotte cleared her throat, and Beth was snapped back to the present. She opened her eyes.

"You had a tough go of it this morning."

Beth opened her mouth to speak, but Charlotte held up her hand, "Let me finish, child. Seems to me that you came in here wanting awfully bad to make a good impression on everybody, and to make sure that everybody knows what the peckin' order is."

"First impressions are so very important," Beth said, cupping her chin in her hand and sighing.

"They certainly are. Which is why I'm suggestin' that you back off a little. You're coming across like a bull in a china shop. You're just like your father. You want to just bull your way through things. Well, sometimes it's better to hang back a little and look around before you start in."

"You don't think I've got what it takes, do you?" She watched the older woman's reaction carefully. Her first impression of Charlotte had been simply a housekeeper,

Denim & Diamonds

kindly and warm, but still, just a housekeeper. And with that country accent she had, she initially came off as a bit of a hick, but the gray-haired woman sitting in front of her was much more than that, and was certainly not an ignorant hick.

Charlotte's hair was pulled up in a loose bun again, but the loose tendrils of gray hair softened her angular face. There were fine lines around her mouth and crows feet at her eyes. Her eyes were bright blue, and she had a way of really looking at the person she was speaking to which made them feel important.

Suddenly, she realized that she really cared whether or not this woman thought she could successfully run the ranch.

Charlotte shook her head, "Didn't say that. But if you want to follow in your daddy's footsteps, take advantage of the people around you. We all love this place like it was ours. We want to see it succeed. This afternoon, have Beau take you on a ride around the ranch. Take a look at what's here."

"Like he's going to want to go anywhere with me after what happened this morning."

"Just go out to the barn and tell him you want to go for a ride. He'll take you," Charlotte stood and headed for the door, "You're the boss, remember?"

After an hour of choosing the clothes and boots she thought would be most appropriate for riding, and gathering her courage, Beth found herself in the barn. It was beautiful – nicer than a lot of houses. The floor was dirt, but it was the cleanest dirt she had ever seen. It looked as though it had been raked recently. To her immediate left was an office, complete with a computer, printer and scanner. Black metal file cabinets lined one wall. There was a fax machine sitting on the cluttered desk next to a multiline phone.

To her right was what must have been the tack room, judging from the numerous saddles sitting on stands and hanging on supports. Straight ahead of her was an aisle leading through the stalls. To her right was a short walkway, which led to another aisle through stalls. The smell of hay and grain and horses wasn't nearly as unpleasant as she had thought it would be. With a smile, she remembered how Beau smelled when he carried her the night of her accident.

She could hear someone talking, and the sound appeared to be coming from the aisle to the right. She walked towards the voice, looking into the stalls as she went. The sliding doors looked heavy, and each one sported a bronze nameplate engraved with the name of the horse. There was also a bronze horsehead hook on each door with a leather halter hanging from it. Beth had to admit, the horses were beautiful, and their soft nickers greeted her as she walked along.

When she reached the end of the aisle, it opened out into a small arena. In the center of the arena, Beau was working with what appeared to be a young horse on a long lead line. The horse was trotting slowly in a circle, and Beau was murmuring encouragement to the animal constantly, moving in a small circle himself. Little puffs of dust were kicked up by its hooves. She stood watching for a few minutes before Beau noticed her.

"What can I do for you, Boss?" he asked, never taking his eyes off the young horse.

"I was wondering if you would take me for a ride and show me around the ranch," she answered as she moved forward and put a booted foot up on the bottom rung of the fence, trying to look casual.

"Yup." Beau slowed the horse to a walk, and then gathered up the lead line. He ran his hand over the horse's neck, and patted him affectionately as the two headed towards her. "Open the gate for me, Boss?"

Her face flushed at the mention of the gate, but she opened it up and held the gate open wide while the cowboy and horse walked through. This was an awkward situation, but she was determined to make the best of it. She was the boss, and she was bound and determined to make sure this

Denim & Diamonds

cowboy remembered that. On the other hand, she was most definitely out of her element here, and she needed him. She followed at a distance as they made their way back down the aisle she had just come through, trying not to stare at the tight Wranglers that were well worn in the seat.

They stopped at a stall and Beau clipped a short rubbery piece hooked on a ring on the wall onto the horse's halter. He lifted the lid on a small plastic stool against the wall and picked out a round rubber brush, which he began rubbing over the horse in little circles.

"This here's a curry." Beau said, then he spoke softly to the horse. Beth wasn't quite sure if he was telling her or the horse what a curry brush was. "You always use the curry on the horse first. They like it. It's like getting your back scratched."

"Oh," Beth said, then stood there awkwardly for a moment, not sure what to say or do. "Do you want me to wait somewhere for you?"

"Nope," the cowboy answered without turning his attention from the horse, "It'll just take me a minute to brush Star down. He's a two year old, out of Snicker by Morning Star. The old man was real happy with him."

Beth nodded, and watched the cowboy carefully. He really did look like a cowboy, from his scuffed leather boots to his well-worn straw cowboy hat. She couldn't help but notice that he filled out his faded blue jeans quite nicely, and his muscles literally rippled under his shirt. His hands were sure and gentle as he groomed the horse and, for a moment, Beth remembered how good it felt when those hands had touched her when he lifted her from her car. Shocked at herself, she gave her head a quick shake to get rid of any thoughts along those lines!

"Problem?" Beau asked, glancing over at Beth.

"No," Beth answered quickly. She frowned when she realized Beau was smiling. Probably laughing at her. She pulled herself up to her full 5'5" and tried to look confident, while inside her stomach was churning as her thoughts turned to riding one of these animals. And of being so close to someone who made her so crazy. She had prided herself on being a professional, a career woman. Then Bob had come along and it had seemed like the time to settle down and get married. Then he fucked her over. After that, she had sworn off men and had turned her attention to her career as an accountant. And then her father had died and she ended up stuck out here at this stupid ranch. And to top it all off, she was going to have to work closely with a cowboy that was the exact opposite of the men she usually dated – the safe, sensible men, who weren't nearly as exciting or romantic as a cowboy.

She couldn't imagine him boinking a secretary at the office, but maybe a roll in the hay . . .

Beau unhooked the horse from the tie, and led him into a stall, where he slipped the halter off. The horse rubbed his face vigorously against the cowboy, who responded with a laugh that was deep and pleasant. A voice from the hay loft above startled Beth.

"Beau, you want me to toss some hay down to Star?"

"That'd be great, Katie, thanks." Beau slid the door closed, then moved down to the next stall and took the leather halter off the hook. "Then come down here and help me get Dingo ready for the Boss."

"Be right there."

Beth felt out of place as she watched the cowboy and the young girl work quickly and easily with the big animals. They shared the same grooming tools, and bantered as they groomed the horses and saddled them up. She wondered if she would ever feel that sense of closeness with another human being. Especially a man as attractive as-

"Here you go," Beau said, breaking her train of thought. She was thankful that he had been concentrating on the task at hand and, hopefully, hadn't noticed the flush creeping up her cheeks. Katie had Dingo saddled and ready in just a few minutes. She watched the gelding (a castrated male, as Katie had so helpfully explained) carefully as

Denim & Diamonds

Beau got his horse saddled. Her horse was gray – dapple gray, Beau had said – and appeared to be ancient. He stood with one hip stuck out and a hind leg up and resting. His nose nearly touched the ground, and Beth was pretty sure he had gone to sleep. Beau's, on the other hand, seemed to be wide-awake. He talked to the horse constantly, and its ears swiveled toward the sound of his master's voice.

Digger was nearly black, and had a white streak down his face. He was muscular and looked as though he was anxious to get going, his feet moving constantly. Beau took pains to position the saddle blanket on the horse, and then lifted the saddle onto the horse and set it carefully down. Beth almost asked why he slid the saddle back a touch, but didn't want to sound stupid. She loved the way the muscles in his arms bulged when he lifted the saddle, and she noticed a small tattoo on his right forearm. Beth had to stop herself from wondering if perhaps the cowboy had a wild side.

Beau and Katie unhooked the horses and led them down the aisle, into the bright June sunshine. The girl talked softly to the gray horse while Beau helped Beth get on him, but disappeared back into the barn as soon as Beth was seated.

Getting up into the saddle was less of a chore than Beth thought it would be, but it was still a challenge to pull herself up and swing her leg over, all while trying to hold onto the reins and the saddle horn, and keeping her balance at the same time. Once up, she wiggled her right foot, but couldn't seem to get her toes lined up with the stirrup. She tensed as Beau took hold of her foot and guided it into the stirrup. His touch was so sure and confident. Nothing half-way about him, Beth thought as she watched him mount his own horse in one fluid motion. He looked at her and smiled, which was terribly disarming and distracting, to Beth's dismay. Sternly, she reminded herself that he was an *employee*, not a date.

"Haven't ever ridden before, have you?" Beau asked. Before Beth could answer, he continued, "And those hacks in the city don't count."

He pulled his horse beside hers and gave her a quick lesson in riding. Beth found herself holding her breath as he leaned next to her, his strong, tanned hands over her pale, trembling ones, showing her how to hold the reins. He smiled at her reassuringly, and she loved his lop-sided smile. She was acutely aware of his leg brushing against hers. They were so close, she could feel his muscles tense as he used his legs to control his horse. His shoulder touched hers, and she could feel him, smell him. He sat back up in his saddle, and looked at Beth. Their eyes met and neither spoke for what seemed like forever, then Beau broke the spell and urged his horse forward.

"Just follow me." He tossed over his shoulder, "We'll go slow. And don't worry about Dingo there. You'll be fine on him. Just do what I told you."

A black and white dog appeared from around the corner of the barn and fell into step with the horses. His fur was long and silky looking, and he looked a lot like the dog in the portrait in the living room.

Beth nodded towards the dog, "Is that one of my father's dogs?"

"Yup. That there's Frank. He's a Border Collie, which is a real smart breed anyway, but he's even smarter than most. Frank didn't let your daddy get too far out of his sight. He's sort of taken up with me since the old man died."

The dog looked up, one ear cocked, at the sound of his name, but he never broke stride. Beth had to admit that he certainly looked more intelligent than the little teacup dogs that some of her neighbors owned, particularly the ones with little bows in their hair who were carried around in little doggie purses.

They rode past the big house and turned right just past the smaller cabin. Beau kept up a running, if brief, description of the ranch. Beth tried to listen as he told her

Denim & Diamonds

what was kept in each pasture, but she couldn't keep her mind off of *him*. He was way too dangerous for her to get involved with. She preferred accountants, lawyers – professionals with a future. This guy was just a cowboy, a ranch hand. A little voice whispered in her head, reminding her, *"But he's the ranch manager."*

Beth frowned, irritated with herself for even thinking that way. He was her employee. She was the boss. And if she had any intention whatsoever of winning her father's challenge and walking away with that money, she'd better focus on the job at hand and quit letting lust control her mind.

"What's wrong?" Beau asked. He had turned in the saddle and was watching Beth closely, his brow furrowed.

"Nothing." Beth answered quickly.

"You sure do frown a lot for nothing being wrong." Beau said, slowing his horse and allowing Dingo to draw even. Beth looked down. Only two or three inches separated her legs from his. She shivered involuntarily.

"And you can't be cold. It's got to be at least 80 degrees out here today." Beau said, his dark brown eyes focused on Beth.

"Not cold. Just nervous I guess," Beth said, as she met his gaze. She managed to hold it for a few seconds, and then broke it, afraid she might give something away with her eyes.

"I don't mean to pry, but you never visited the ranch before, did you?" Beau asked as the horses continued to walk along at an easy pace.

"No. I've lived in Kansas City all my life. My parents separated when I was in high school. He moved down here, and I stayed in the city with Mother. When it was time for visitation, my father came to the City to see me. Then I got caught up in college and a career, and just didn't have time to get out here." Beth said, surprising herself that she revealed so much to a stranger. She was enjoying the ride though, and found herself relaxing. The rhythm of the horse's walk was soothing, as was the sound

31

Elle Robb

of their hooves on the dirt path and the creak of the leather. Little wispy clouds floated across the blue sky. And she loved the orderliness and cleanliness of the white wooden fencing that crisscrossed the rolling hills.

"The old man loved it out here. He was really in his element." Beau's voice grew soft, "I miss him."

Suddenly, Beth's horse snorted furiously and reared up, throwing her forward. The saddle horn dug deep into her stomach, forcing the air out. The leather reins slid through her hands, burning and searing. She grabbed for mane, and held on for dear life. The next minute or so was a blur, but she was vaguely aware that her feet were no longer in the stirrups, and Dingo was jerking wildly from side to side, still whinnying frantically. She saw Beau was reaching for the bridle. Finally, everything came to a stop. She wasn't sure who was breathing harder, her or her horse.

"There was a rattlesnake. Scared Dingo," Beau sounded out of breath, too. "You okay, Boss?"

Beth turned to look at the man who had now saved her twice. Her stomach hurt horribly where the saddle horn had dug into her. She felt dizzy and scared, but was trying to take deep breaths and stay calm. She kept telling herself to keep it together, make a good impression. She started to tell him she didn't feel good, but to her utter horror, she threw up and then everything started to go dark.

Denim & Diamonds

<u>CHAPTER FIVE</u>

Beau leaned forward and caught his boss, just as her eyes rolled up into her head and she lurched toward him. He took a deep breath and tried to ignore the fact that both of them – and the horses, for that matter – were in dire need of a shower. The saddle was definitely going to need a good cleaning. Good grief, what a frickin' mess. He kept a firm grip on Beth's arm and urged his horse forward. Dingo plodded along, just as Beau hoped he would. Beth wobbled a bit in her seat, but Beau was pretty sure they'd make it back to the barn okay if they just went slow. He sighed and shook his head. Though he had lots of ideas about what his new boss would be like, this was certainly not a scenario he had pictured.

Beau glanced over at Beth. When he first saw her, right after the wreck, he had been immediately attracted to her. She had seemed like the stereotypical damsel in distress, a true woman. He was so tired of all the stupid feminists in the world. He was pretty sure he had dated every feminist in the Moscow area. Janice, his on-and-off girlfriend, was a perfect example. She never let him get the door for her. In fact, she often held the door for him. Whenever they went out, she insisted on going Dutch. It just got old. Beau was well aware of the fact that he was getting older. He was starting to think about settling down. When he did settle down, he wanted a woman that was a

33

woman – a girl his mama would approve of. Someone who was soft and warm, and who made him feel like a man. When he had pulled this little redhead from that wrecked car, he had felt every bit the hero. She had snuggled up to him when he carried her to the truck, her breath tickling his neck and sending chills down his spine.

But what could he offer a woman like Beth? She was used to life in the city, the finer things in life. He was a cowboy, who barely made it from paycheck to paycheck and who was thankful room and board was part of the deal here at the Domino. He wore blue jeans, she wore diamonds . . . and denim and diamonds just don't mix.

Beau frowned, reminding himself that the biggest problem was that the woman he rescued had turned out to be his new boss. He and the old man had been close. The old man had taken him in and treated him like a son – Pickard had never really gotten over losing his only son during Desert Storm- and treated Beau like a partner in running the ranch. Beau had been shocked to discover that the old man had left the ranch to his daughter. On those rare occasions when the old man had talked about his daughter, it had been as if he didn't understand her and didn't particularly want to understand her. He described his daughter as being "driven" and "obstinate". To hear him talk, this wisp of a woman had fought him tooth and nail when he had insisted that she follow in his footsteps and attend the University of Missouri-Columbia. She had wanted to go to a small, private college, but since he was paying for it, he got his way. He was disappointed that his daughter showed no interest in his life, but he had been proud of her.

Beau remembered with a smile the night the old man had asked him to join him in the library for a toast. The occasion had been Beth making partner in the accounting firm. Yes, he was proud of his daughter. But that didn't give him the right to leave Domino Ranch to her. Beau caught himself. Actually, it did. She was the old man's flesh and blood. Beau was just a hired hand and, he

Denim & Diamonds

reminded himself, a good friend. But wealthy people don't leave piles of money and valuable property to their friends. They keep it in the family. Beau knew what the Will said. And he had no intention of falling for a woman who was going to leave as soon as she collected her million bucks, or of helping her win that money. And a lady like her sure wouldn't stick around for a cowboy like him.

Beth groaned, pulling Beau back to reality and he pulled back on the reins. She groaned again, and held a hand to her stomach. Her eyes fluttered open, showing slivers of green as bright as the first grass of spring, and Beau couldn't help but notice how long her eyelashes were. Slowly, she focused on him.

"Oh, God, I feel awful," Beth said. She sniffed, then looked down. She groaned again, and her pale cheeks flushed red. "I got sick."

"Yup," Beau answered with a smile, "You got sick."

"The saddle horn caught me in the stomach," Beth said, looking rather vulnerable again. "I remember now. The horse reared up . . . I tried so hard not to get sick. I'm so embarrassed."

"Not a problem. Everybody gets sick at one time or another." Beau said. He looked towards the cluster of buildings directly in front of them, so he wouldn't have to look at those incredible green eyes. He gave himself a mental shake – it had been way too long since he'd been with a woman if he was feeling attracted to someone who had just thrown up all over herself. "Do you feel up to riding the rest of the way?"

"I can make it," Beth said softly. The two urged their horses forward. "I'm sorry. I know I smell."

"You certainly do!" Beau laughed out loud, "At least we're out here in the open, so it's bearable."

Beth smiled gratefully at him, and he felt his resolve to not fall for her melting. Now that it was just the two of them, she seemed nice enough. She had made a mistake this morning, but he imagined that most people who don't grow up around a farm or ranch probably have no idea about closing gates. Maybe he was being too tough on her and expecting too much of her. After all, she'd just gotten here. And she hadn't thrown her weight around too much. The two continued towards the barn in a companionable silence, listening to the soft clip-clop of the horses' hooves on the path and the creak of the saddle leather. A hawk soared across the sky, birds chirped in the trees, and a dog barked in the distance. Frank answered with a soft woof.

They reached the buildings and followed the curve of the path. Beau heard Beth take a sharp breath. He looked over and was surprised to see that she was pale as a ghost. She was staring straight ahead. He followed her gaze and saw a boxy, black Mercedes parked next to his Silverado. Beau turned to Beth, his eyebrows raised.

"Friend of yours?" he asked.

"I wouldn't say that exactly," she replied, a grim look on her face. Her lips were pressed together. Beau urged his horse towards the barn, and Dingo followed. They stopped at the old-fashioned hitching post just outside the barn. Beth waited until Beau dismounted, watching his every move. He could feel her eyes on him. She dismounted, trying to keep from getting any messier on the way down. Beau took the reins and looked his new boss up and down.

"Want to hose off in the barn?" he asked. Beth met his gaze and held her head high. Beau watched her and thought, *hmmm, the dragon lady is back.*

"I will not hose off in the barn like an animal," she retorted. She started towards the house, but paused and looked over her shoulder. "Um, what about the saddle?"

"Don't worry, I'll take care of it." Beau answered, as he angrily pulled the saddle from his horse. She absolutely infuriated him. He'd just start to think he might be able to work with her, and then she'd snap back to an absolutely infuriating beast of a woman. He turned his attention to the task at hand.

Denim & Diamonds

"You and Ms. Pickard go for a ride?" Katie asked, startling Beau.

"Yup," Beau answered, taking the halter Katie offered him and slipping it over Digger's neck.

"What's she like?" Katie asked.

"She's a witch. A cold, heartless witch," Beau answered. Katie shrugged and turned her attention to the horse Beth had ridden.

"Hey, what's all over Dingo?" Katie persisted with the questions. Her nose wrinkled, "Yuck! He stinks!"

"The boss lady got sick." Beau said. Katie turned to look at Beau, her hand perched on her hip. She peeked around Beau's horse and watched Beth going around the corner of the main house, then looked back at Beau. He focused on the horse and ignored the girl until she finally shrugged and led Dingo towards the washing stall.

Beth marched towards the side of the house, knowing that her employees were watching her, talking about her, laughing about her. She was desperately hoping she could sneak in the back door and make it to her suite, preferably without running into anyone. And desperately hoping that that car in the driveway did not belong to who she thought it did.

At the side door to the kitchen, Beth kicked her boots off and slipped inside, trying to be as quiet as possible.

"My goodness, child! What happened to you?" Charlotte popped up from her seat at the big table and rushed towards Beth. Her hand immediately went to her face, covering her nose, "Oh, dear, you stink to high heaven!"

"Thank you for noticing," Beth said through clenched teeth. "Can you please excuse me while I go clean up?"

"Hello, Beth," Beth froze when she heard that voice. That horribly cultured, smooth voice.

37

"What are you doing here, Bob?" Beth asked, looking past Charlotte to face the dark haired man sitting at the table.

"Is that any way to greet your fiance?" Bob asked as he pushed his chair out and stretched up, not quite reaching the 6' that he claimed to be. Charlotte stepped back, looking like she didn't know whether to offer the two tea and cookies, or retreat and leave them alone. Beth figured she'd probably stay, to make sure there wasn't any blood spilled.

"You are not my fiance. It's over," Beth said firmly. She turned to Charlotte, "Please see Mr. Worthington out. He is not welcome here."

"I will see myself out. But we're not through here. There are items that we must discuss, Elizabeth."

Beth seethed. She hated the fact that he called her by her given name when he was angry with her, as if she were an errant child. She took a deep breath and said with all the self-confidence she could muster, given the fact that she was covered in vomit and couldn't get the mental image of Bob boinking a secretary out of her mind, "Fine. But not here, not now. I will meet you in town at the café at 8:00 tonight."

Charlotte cleared her throat and whispered, "The café closes at 8."

Beth bit her lower lip, "Meet me there at 7. We can discuss whatever we need to discuss in an hour." With that, she stepped around Charlotte and Bob and headed for the sanctuary of her room. She couldn't take another moment of smelling herself, or looking at that bastard.

CHAPTER SIX

That afternoon, Beth took extra care with her appearance. She picked a pair of her designer jeans that fit her like a glove, and chose a red silk camisole which peeked out from under a black short sleeved shirt. She cleaned her rings until the diamonds and pearls sparkled. A black clip held her hair back, and diamond studs and a plain gold chain finished the look. She knew it was silly, but she desperately wanted to make Bob want her so she could rebuff him. She didn't know what he was up to, but he was definitely up to something. She knew him too well. And he certainly hadn't come up here to make amends and ask for her forgiveness. That wasn't Bob's style.

Beth pulled up to the café in Charlotte's Suburban, taking a parking space two down from Bob's Mercedes. Even though she'd only been at the ranch a couple of days, she had already started to see the silliness of the conspicuous consumption lifestyle that Bob lived – and that she had been living. She glanced up just as a familiar Chevy pickup drove past. She waved at Beau, but he was staring straight ahead and didn't see her. She shrugged and went into the café. What the ranch foreman did on his time was his business.

Beau cursed when he saw Beth look up just as he was driving by. He hoped she thought he just hadn't seen her. When Charlotte had first suggested that Beau follow Beth to make sure she was okay, he had balked. The idea of

39

sneaking around and spying on the boss lady and her fiance wasn't his idea of a good time. Beau wasn't sure what Beth would do if she caught him following her around, but he didn't think she'd thank him for it. But then Charlotte had told Beau about how rude and mean that man had seemed. She'd even gone so far as to describe him as a snake. So, Beau found himself pulling up to the curb in front of the hardware store, hoping that Beth hadn't noticed him stopping. He flipped off the radio, cutting Brooks and Dunn off in the middle of their Boot Scootin'. That was okay. Didn't really fit his mood anyway.

Beau walked down the sidewalk, trying to look casual, until he reached the café. He peeked in the front window just as Beth was approaching a table where a dark-haired man was seated. The guy's face was clean shaven and his hairline was receding. He wore black-rimmed glasses, and had on a dark pink dress shirt. Beau laughed at that, wearing a dress shirt in the Moscow café was pretty much a dead giveaway that you didn't belong, and wearing a pink shirt was liable to earn you a knuckle sandwich.

Beau frowned when the man stood up and pulled Beth's chair out for her. He was short, just a few inches taller than Beth. Beth smiled politely and sat down. She was absolutely stunning, all dressed up like that. Her back was to the front window, but Beau could see her companion just fine. He fought the urge to go in and join them. That probably wasn't what Charlotte intended. And that probably wouldn't win him any brownie points with the boss lady, either.

Beau continued to watch, leaning casually against the building and trying to look nonchalant. He lit a cigarette and took a long drag on it. A couple of people spoke to him on their way out of the café, but he told them he was waiting for someone. He hoped he was believable, but Jack Carson looked at him strangely when he snuck another look in the window while they were talking about how the yearlings were looking. Finally, Jack shrugged and walked away, shaking his head.

Denim & Diamonds

It looked as though the man had ordered for both he and Beth, but Beth wasn't eating. What really bugged Beau was that Beth kept leaning in close to her boyfriend. That intimate crap just made Beau's blood boil. He tried to tell himself that he was irritated that the boss lady would be stupid enough to stay involved with someone who treated her like dirt. But then he began to wonder if she looked at this guy like she'd looked at him that first night. And he remembered how she felt, light as a feather in his arms. Did this guy know every inch of Beth's body? Did he hold her close while they slept? Did she lay her head against his chest?

Beau turned away, cursing himself for thinking that way. After all, she was his boss. Nothing more. He had no right to think about her that way. She seemed perfectly happy in there with her rich boyfriend, and she'd probably run right back to him and his Mercedes after she collected her million bucks. Beau was sure he'd never see her again. The ranch was just something she had to put up with in order to get the money her daddy had left her. It wasn't like she really cared if the ranch made it or not. It wasn't like she cared about him.

Beau peeked in again, and saw the rich guy holding Beth's hand across the table. She was still leaning close, and they were completely engrossed with one another. It looked as though they weren't aware of anyone else in the café. They made quite the couple – everyone inside was stealing glances at the two lovebirds.

A door opened down the street, music and laughter spilling out as two people walked out of the tavern. It was urban cowboy night, and every drunk in town would be riding the mechanical bull. That was always entertaining. Beau sighed and flicked his cigarette down. He crushed the butt with the heel of his boot and headed for the Come On Inn.

Inside the café, Beth yanked her hand away and hissed at Bob, "I told you, you are not getting the ring back.

I discussed it with my lawyer and since you fucked around on me, I get to keep it."

"You broke off the engagement. My lawyer says *I* get it back." Bob said through his whitened, capped teeth.

"I wouldn't have broken off the engagement if everyone at the firm hadn't been passing around the video of you and your secretary doing it on the conference room table," Beth said, her voice rising.

"Let's be reasonable," Bob said slowly, "Let's start this conversation over again. I don't want this engagement broken off. I want to marry you."

Beth laughed, but there was no laughter in her eyes, "No, you don't. You want to marry my father's money."

Bob's eyes opened wide, "I don't know what you're talking about, Elizabeth. You have no right to talk to me like that."

"Don't scold me, you bastard!" Beth shouted, standing up so quickly her chair fell over. "It is over between us. Do you hear me? Over!"

Beth spun around and fled, her face burning. She kept her eyes straight ahead, avoiding the glances of the other patrons in the restaurant and desperately hoping that none of them were employees of the ranch. Behind her, she heard Bob shout something, but she just kept going, out the door and across the street and into the park. By the time she collapsed on a wooden park bench, hot tears were streaming down her cheeks.

She just let it go, really let it go, for the first time since she found out about Bob and the secretary. She had tried so hard to deal with the whole situation methodically and practically, but honestly, it just plain hurt. It hurt so badly to think that the man who she had planned to spend her life with, and who had seemed like perfect husband material, had turned out to be such scum. Such lousy, good-for-nothing scum. She wrapped her arms around herself, and rocked back and forth, letting the sobs rack her body and then, slowly, her crying let up and the tears stopped flowing. Finally, her breath was coming in ragged little hiccups, but she actually felt better.

She sat up on the bench and leaned her head back. The clouds had cleared up and the moon was nearly full. The sky was dotted with stars, and it reminded Beth of going to the planetarium as a child. She smiled, remembered how she and Ian had held hands when the lights went down. Sure, having a little brother was a pain sometimes, but most of the time she had to admit that she really missed him. He had nearly broken her hand he squeezed so tight when the "Big Bang" theory was explained – and had nearly broken her eardrum when he screamed at the sound! She pulled her sweatshirt closer around herself and tried to remember as many of the constellations as she could.

Less than a block away, Beau had taken a seat at the bar in the Come On Inn. He was drinking a Busch and watching a young buck who was celebrating his 21st birthday try to ride the mechanical bull. Fluffy had been nice, which was unusual for Fluffy, and had started the bull on the easiest setting. Even at that setting, the kid couldn't stay on the bull more than two seconds. He probably should have tried riding the bull before starting on his free shots.

"You gonna ride the bull tonight, Sugar?" Beau turned to find Janice taking the empty seat next to him. He shook his head and looked back at the kid who was climbing back on the bull yet again.

"He just doesn't know when to give up, does he?" Janice asked. She motioned to the bartender and ordered up two more beers. She slid one in front of Beau. "Kind of like me, huh?"

"What?" Beau asked, tossing back the last of his beer.

"Guess I don't know when to give up either. I haven't give up on you yet, have I?" Janice said as she leaned towards Beau, giving him a perfect view of her cleavage. Beau raised his eyebrows, then clanked his bottle against hers.

"Here's to people that don't give up," he said. He motioned to the bartender to set up two more beers.

Beau wasn't sure how much time had passed, but there were a lot of bottles in front of him and Fluffy had turned off the mechanical bull. He and Janice had been dancing. Well, standing and moving to the music, he thought with a smile. He was feeling a little fuzzy and decided it was time to get a little fresh air.

"Be careful, man," Fluffy said, waving to the two on their way out. Beau nodded and threw his arm over Janice's shoulder. She had an arm around his waist. The two burst out the door, singing "Friends in Low Places" at the top of their lungs. Just as they finished their song, Beau leaned back against his truck to steady himself. Janice leaned against him, her body pressed tight against his, and reached up to put her arms around his neck. She pulled his head down and kissed him. He hesitated, and then kissed back, feeling warm and fuzzy. He pushed her away gently.

"I don't think either one of us had better drive just now," Beau said, slurring his words.

"What 'cha want to do then?" Janice asked suggestively.

Beau grabbed Janice by the hand and headed across the street. "Let's sit. Just sit. On the gabezo – I mean, the gazebo."

From the park bench in the shadow of the big oak tree, Beth watched silently. She had been enjoying the peace and quiet in the dark park, lost in memories and thoughts, and reflecting on her life as a single woman. As if it weren't bad enough to be alone, she now had to watch the two lovebirds make out in the park. She wasn't about to move and draw attention to herself, so she just sat there, watching and thinking. She watched the way Beau touched the brunette. The way he stroked her hair. The way he cradled her in his arms when he kissed her. Beau seemed like such a rough, cowboy-type. But he was definitely

Denim & Diamonds

capable of passion. And passion was something that Beth had never experienced before. Bob certainly wouldn't be romantic with her in the moonlight in the park . . . But Beth could well imagine what it would be like to be held in Beau's arms, to have his strong hands stroke her hair, to feel his lips take her own, to feel his hard body pressed against hers . . .

Elle Robb

CHAPTER SEVEN

Life at the ranch settled into a somewhat comfortable existence over the next few weeks, though the relative peace was punctuated by occasional calls from Bob. Beau disappeared on Friday and Saturday nights, likely spending his time with the brunette from the park. Charlotte and Beth were getting comfortable with each other, getting to know each other and usually spending pleasant evenings watching television together. Katie joined them frequently, sometimes spending the night in the "pink room".

Beth finally her car back, nearly as good as new, had finally moved her belongings from suitcases and hung them in the guest bedroom, and was learning the ins and outs of managing the day-to-day business of running the ranch. She rose at the crack of dawn with everyone else, ate breakfast with her employees around the big oak table – Charlotte made incredibly good strawberry pancakes – and then headed to the barn with Beau to help with the morning chores.

As she quickly learned, Beau had been much more than just the ranch foreman. He had been her father's right hand man, confidante and most trusted advisor. Initially, she had been surprised that the rough and tumble cowboy she saw was actually a very astute businessman. The two spent many hours in the office in the barn, poring over pedigrees, breeding records, sales records and health

Denim & Diamonds

records for the horses. Beau was patient with her, and explained why things had been run the way they had.

When Jonathan Pickard had bought the farm, it had been a ramshackle mess. The former owner had won the lottery, built everything up very quickly, then lost interest in the place. The timing was perfect. Beth's father had made a fortune in the stock market investing in dot com ventures, had gotten out just before the bubble burst, and was looking for a place to retire. He had rebuilt everything from the ground up, and this was now a first-class horse breeding and training operation, specializing in cutting horses. The top rodeo cowboys in the nation came to the Domino Ranch when they were in need of a horse that would win.

Beth and Beau also spent many hours with the horses. While he trained the young horses, she could often be found sitting on the top rung of the fence, watching carefully. Frank, her father's border collie and constant companion during his time at the ranch, took to sitting at Beth's feet whenever Beau was working in the round pen. At first, the other ranch hands had laughed at Beth because she took copious notes. They thought she was writing letters to some boyfriend back home. In fact, she kept detailed notes about the training of each and every horse on the ranch.

She was determined to know the business inside and out – and that meant knowing the horses. Beth had no experience with horses. No experience with animals, for that matter, but she caught on quick. Frank obviously approved of her, and the three-legged calico cat was always close by. Beth was able to make suggestions that really came in handy. The first few times she made a suggestion, Beau scoffed at her, not about to take the word of a city girl.

Then, one day, she commented to him that Buckaroo, a two year old sorrel gelding that Beau had been working, seemed to work better when he was worked clockwise. She thought maybe it was his sight – she told

47

Beau it seemed as though the horse was looking oddly at the rail when he was being worked counterclockwise. Once it was brought to his attention, he realized she was right. They got the horse back in the stall and looked him over carefully and, sure enough, something was different about his right eye. He called the vet out and Doc Spiner confirmed that Buckaroo did indeed have only partial vision in that eye. After that, Beau paid a little more attention when Beth made an observation. She was aware of the fact that he now listened to her and took her more seriously, but she didn't make a big deal out of it. She was well aware that the ranch hands would probably be afraid she would get a big head after Beau told them what had happened with Buckaroo.

Socially, things had settled down a bit around the ranch, too. Bob still called every now and then, using the excuse of questions about her accounting clients, and had sent flowers on more than one occasion. Beth had agreed to meet him in town a couple of times in order to finish up some business dealings for the firm. As far as she was concerned, it was business only and she ignored his advances. She knew that he could eventually get nasty, but was sure she could handle him. And, honestly, it gave her an excuse for some semblance of a social life. And kept her mind off of Beau in any sort of romantic sense. Or, that was what she told herself, anyway.

Beau saw Janice occasionally. It was tough not to, since it was rodeo season and she was a rodeo bunny. He tolerated her, and considered her a somewhat pleasant distraction. He hated to admit that he was attracted to his boss, and having someone to date helped him to keep his mind – and body – occupied.

One evening, Beau found himself knocking around the small house by himself, with only Frank to keep him company. Rusty and Joe, the other ranch hands he shared the little house with, had gone over to a neighboring ranch for a night of poker, but Beau had begged off. He didn't like spending too much social time with the men he was supposed to supervise. Sometimes it was hard to be effective if the line had been blurred too much, or if they got too chummy with him. There was a light rain coming down, so he didn't want to go outside and ride or go for a walk with Frank like he would normally do. He checked the fridge and found it nearly empty, so he and Frank headed to the main house to see if Charlotte had any of her famous oatmeal cookies laying around.

"Hello?" he called as he stepped through the kitchen door. The kitchen had been cleaned up, and the table was set for breakfast.

"In here, Beau!" Charlotte called from the other room. He could hear laughter coming from the living room, so he grabbed a cookie from the teddy bear cookie jar on the counter and poked his head around the corner. Charlotte was in the easy chair, wrapped in her terry cloth robe and crocheting a pale blue afghan. Beth, in gray sweats and an oversized Kansas City Chiefs sweatshirt, was curled up on one side of the big brown sectional. The little calico cat was perched on the back of the sofa, her tail moving lazily. There was a big bowl of popcorn sitting on the coffee table, and there were two beers sitting on coasters.

"Hey!" Beth said, "Come on in and have a seat. We're just getting ready to start a movie."

"Absolutely," Charlotte chimed in, "Grab yourself a beer and join us."

Beau stood there for a moment, trying to decide what to do. Popcorn sounded good. A cold beer sounded better. Just then, lightning flashed and thunder boomed.

"You know, if you're sure you don't mind, I think I will join you two," he said, ducking back to the kitchen to grab a Busch from the refrigerator.

After he got his beer and took a seat on the other side of the sectional from Beth, Charlotte reached over to dim the lights. Frank hopped up on the sectional, taking the corner. Beth hit play on the remote and the movie started. Beau groaned when he realized it was When Harry Met

Sally. Billy Crystal was funny, and Meg Ryan was cute, but this was a chick flick!

Beth looked at Beau and giggled, "Didn't know what you were in for, did ya?"

Beau took a swig of beer and shrugged, "Even this beats sitting in my house by myself watching reruns of Friends."

Beth looked at him and raised her beer. "To Friends."

"To Friends," he said, as he raised his own beer to salute his boss. She had become a friend to him since she arrived, but that would only work if he was able to ignore her full lips, her round breasts and her firm behind. He reminded himself that he had seen her with her boyfriend. He knew they had met for dinner a couple of times (let's face it – in a town the size of Moscow, everyone knew when old man Pickard's daughter was having dinner with that high-class guy with the Mercedes).

Beau took another swig of beer and sat back to watch the movie. After a few minutes, he reached over to get a handful of popcorn, and his hand brushed the warm softness of Beth's hand. They both pulled their hands back, embarrassed at the touch. Beau cleared his throat, then drained his beer and headed to the kitchen for another.

Beth settled back into her corner of the soft sofa and watched Beau as he walked quickly from the room. The way he filled out his faded jeans was absolutely incredible. There were so many times when she would catch herself just staring at him when he was working the horses. She would completely forget that she was supposed to be taking notes. There was something about the way he appeared so rough on the outside, yet he was so gentle and patient with the horses. And he and his dog seemed to share a special language. It was really something to see him work a pen full of cattle – it was a three part team – Beau, Digger and Frank worked together better than most humans did.

Beth stole a glance at Beau as he appeared from the kitchen with a fresh beer, and wondered what it was he saw

Denim & Diamonds

in the woman he was seeing. Beth smiled as she remembered how Charlotte had referred to Janice in a most unflattering way as a "rodeo bunny", hopping around after cowboys. He took his seat, then sat stroking his moustache with one hand, and stroking his dog's silky fur with the other, his beer balanced between his legs. That was someplace she simply could not allow her mind to go. The calico hopped down from the back of the sofa, made two turns and settled into a ball. Beth sighed and turned her attention back to the movie.

Beth caught herself blushing when she realized what was coming up in the movie – the famous diner scene where Meg Ryan fakes an orgasm. She stared straight ahead during the scene, careful not to look at Beau in his faded blue jeans.

Across the room, Beau was staring at the television trying very hard not to look at Beth in her sweats that made her look so comfortable and warm. In the easy chair, Charlotte had begun snoring loudly. Her crochet hook dropped to the floor with a tinny thud. Beth smiled and looked at Beau, just as he looked at her. He was smiling his crooked smile, trying not to laugh out loud so as not to wake Charlotte up from her deep slumber. Frank's tail thumped happily against the sofa cushions. Slowly, their smiles faded as they stared at each other. Thoughts tumbled in their minds, but neither spoke.

Beau thought Beth was one of the most beautiful women he'd ever seen, and all he could think about was what she would look like if he could just get rid of those gray sweats. But she was his boss, and she was rich. He couldn't allow himself to think of herself . . . that way.

Beth thought Beau was one of the sexiest men she'd ever seen. All she could think about was how it would feel to have those strong arms wrapped around her. But he was her employee, and she couldn't compete with a buxom young blonde that understood the cowboy life. She just couldn't allow herself to think that she might ever be anything more than a boss to him.

BAM! BAM! BAM! Charlotte jumped and knocked her beer to the floor. Frank jumped to his feet, barking furiously at the door. Beth blinked and Beau stood up.

BAM! BAM! BAM!

"Heavens to Betsy! One of you answer that door and stop that God-awful poundin', for Pete's sake!" Charlotte groused, trying to salvage her beer and mop up the rest of it with her napkin.

Denim & Diamonds

CHAPTER EIGHT

Beau flung upon the door, and his chin dropped when he saw the woman framed in the doorway. He squinted, frowned, then smiled. The cat jumped from the sofa and hid under the coffee table. Frank stood on the sofa, tail waggin and his front feet on the back so he could get a better view of the door.

"Get in here out of that weather, Aunt Flo!" he said as he stepped back to allow the woman into the living room. A gust of wind and rain followed her in like a shadow.

Beth and Charlotte stood to greet their visitor. She was easily a foot shorter than Beau, and her long thin fingers hinted that she was wiry, but it was hard to tell because her frame was hidden beneath layers of brightly colored clothes. She had on two skirts, one purple, and one lime green, peeking out from beneath. Both skirts nearly reached her red tennis shoes, but didn't quite hide the red and white striped socks she was sporting. The skirts were topped with what appeared to be pink thermal undershirt, covered by a black Ozzy Osbourne t-shirt. A map of wrinkles creased her face, and her skin was the color of old paper. Beth gaze bounced back and forth between Beau and the woman – their complexions were different, but they had the same perfectly straight nose and square chin. It was impossible to tell if they had the same hair color, though

53

Beth suspected the woman may have had dark brown hair at some point – now it was bright red, cut short in a pixie cut with little points curling forward in front of her ears. She was very bright, and Beth figured that was why a low growl was rumbling in Frank's throat.

Charlotte recovered first, "You must be Beau's Aunt Flo! I've heard so much about you over the years!"

Charlotte excused herself to get a towel and Beau introduced his new boss to the woman who raised him. He quickly explained that his parents had been killed in a freak accident at a carnival when he was just a child, and that his mother's sister had taken him in and raised him. Beth stood nodding, not sure what to say, and tried to imagine this flamboyant woman as a mother figure. She just couldn't quite get that mental image fixed in her mind, as hard as she tried.

Charlotte returned with a thirsty towel and Aunt Flo quickly dried off. Charlotte told them to have a seat and she headed for the kitchen for refreshments. To her, every occasion required food and drink – preferably cookies and hot cocoa. Beau and Aunt Flo had sat down on the sofa, both sitting sideways so they could face each other. Beau looked surprised and excited and happy. Beth didn't think she'd ever seen him smile for more than a few seconds since she'd known him, but that lop-sided grin had been glued to his face ever since he'd opened the door. Beth felt like an intruder and escaped to the kitchen, under the guise of helping Charlotte prepare some hot cocoa.

"Beau seems a lot different than his aunt, doesn't he?" Beth asked Charlotte as they waited for the water in the tea kettle to heat up.

"Yes, different," Charlotte answered slowly. "Beau has had a rough life, and I think his Aunt Flo has been the only constant in his life. But he doesn't see her very often any more. This is the first time she's come here, to my recollection."

"But hasn't Beau lived here at the ranch for about ten years now?" Beth asked.

Denim & Diamonds

"At least. He's gone to visit his aunt a couple of times when she happened to be passing through. But she's never come here before."

Their conversation was ended by the whistling of the tea kettle. Charlotte filled the cups with hot water, Beth added the cocoa mix and stirred. Charlotte carefully balanced the cups on the serving tray and headed for the living room. Beth took the plate of Charlotte's famous oatmeal cookies and followed. Beau and Flo had been leaning close, but they sat up straight when Charlotte and Beth entered.

The four of them sat together, eating and drinking, and Charlotte tried to make small talk. Things seemed just a little stressed, though, and Beth wasn't quite sure what to make of the situation. She noticed that Beau's grin had faded, and his brow was slightly furrowed. He kept glancing at his aunt with a worried look. His aunt, however, seemed to be trying too hard to be happy. Her laughter was a bit forced, and she was too bubbly. Beth realized though that, given the way Flo looked, too bubbly might be her usual demeanor.

"So, Flo, what brings you to the Moscow area?" Beth asked.

"Work. I'm a trucker. Just passing through and thought I'd stop to see my favorite nephew." Flo grinned widely, and Beth noticed that one of her top teeth was missing.

"Well, we're so glad you did," Charlotte said, "I will fix up one of the guest bedrooms for you. You able to stay a few days?"

"She can stay in the spare room in the small house," Beau answered quickly, "It's empty since Gabe quit a couple of months ago. And I'm sure Aunt Flo won't be able to stay more than one night."

"I might be able to stay a few nights," Flo said, still grinning from ear to ear. Beth noticed an oatmeal cookie peeking from Flo's skirt pocket.

"But, Aunt Flo," Beau said firmly, lowering his chin and looking straight at Flo, "We don't want to put you behind schedule."

"Oh, I'll be fine. No hurry at all on this load. Don't have to be to Pittsburgh until the end of the week," Flo said as she grabbed another cookie.

Beau stood abruptly, "I'm sure you've had a long drive today, and it sounds like the rain's let up out there. Better take advantage of the lull. Let's head over to my house and get you settled in."

Charlotte and Beth stood awkwardly, trading a suspicious glance before they said their goodbyes to Beau and his aunt. Beau took his aunt by the arm and was firmly guiding her through the kitchen and out the side door. Frank was following at Beau's heels, the thick black hair still standing up on his neck. The two women stood there for a few minutes, both wondering what had just happened. Finally, Charlotte shrugged, sat back down in her easy chair and pushed the play button on the remote.

"Best we just finish our movie. Beau will tell us what's going on in his own good time," she said to no one in particular.

Beth took her usual spot on the sofa. The three-legged cat appeared from under the table and hopped up beside her. She turned three times, then curled up in the crook of Beth's legs.

Outside, Beau stopped for a moment to admire Flo's semi. It was a pink Peterbilt with a sleeper. A pretty nice rig. Much nicer than the old green one she had. It hadn't had a sleeper, if he remembered correctly. Flo climbed up and disappeared in the cab for a moment, then tossed out a worn duffel bag. Beau threw it over this shoulder and held out his hand to help her down.

"You always were a good boy, Beau," Flo said with a smile. "Well, usually, anyway."

"That's behind me," Beau hissed. "I don't want to hear anything about the past. Let's just get inside and get you settled in. For tonight only."

Denim & Diamonds

"Now is that any way to treat the woman who raised you?" Flo asked innocently.

Beau just shook his head and headed for the small house, with Frank at his heels. Flo followed, looking around as she went. She could barely make out the shape of the barn, and she seemed to be listening to the horses moving on the other side of the white fence.

"That Chevy pickup is pretty nice," Flo commented, nodding towards the Silverado, "Whose is it?"

"Mine," Beau answered with a frown, "And don't even be thinking what you're thinking. I thought you had changed. You were going to straighten out."

Once inside, Beau headed straight for the spare bedroom and dropped the bag on the hardwood floor. Without a word, he pulled a set of cotton sheets from the cedar chest at the foot of the twin bed and began making the bed. Flo headed for the small bathroom that connected the spare bedroom to Beau's room. She closed the door with a firm thud. When she returned, Beau was angrily stuffing the goose down pillow into the pillowcase.

"What is wrong with you, Beau?" Flo asked as she perched on the side of the bed.

"What's wrong is that I have tried really hard to build a normal life for myself, and I've been doing a pretty good job of it. And now you show up here, and all sorts of memories came flooding back. I'm different now, Aunt Flo." Beau sighed heavily, and pulled on his moustache.

"You're different all right, Beau." Flo said, grinning that wild grin. "But you can't run from who you are."

"I'm not running from who I am," Beau said firmly, "Who I am is the foreman on this ranch. It's a good job and I've got a good life now."

"You don't need a good job, Beau. People like us-"

"No! I am not 'like us' anymore. There *is* no us." Beau said. He went through the bathroom and paused to look at Flo before he closed the door. "I love you, but I'm different now. I don't do that stuff anymore."

He stalked into his room, angry and frustrated, both with himself and with his aunt. Seeing her brought back so many memories. He had been so young, he barely remembered his parents, who'd both been killed when the Scrambler had flown apart at the local carnival. He had been so angry with them because they were riding all the fun rides and he was stuck standing on the sidelines watching. He was there – and he could still see the car flying in slow motion through the air, he could hear the screams of his parents and the others that had been riding. He saw them smash into the fun house, and heard the crunch of metal as it collapsed after the impact. He had nightmares about that for years. Still did, every now and then.

And he remembered how it had seemed that no one wanted him. How he had been shuffled around from house to house for what seemed like forever, but had actually been only a few days. Then Aunt Flo had come to the funeral. No one in the family wanted anything to do with her. Beau had liked the fact that she didn't care what anyone thought of her. She had been the only one to put her arm around him and just be there for him during the funeral. Especially during that horrible graveside service, with the empty holes opened wide like toothless mouths, waiting to swallow his parents up. She had gathered him up in her arms then, in a big bear hug, and asked him if he wanted to stay with her, to keep her company. He had nodded solemnly and, that afternoon, he packed a bag with his most important possessions, his scrapbook, his copy of The Black Stallion, and his model horses. When Flo pulled out of town that night in her big rig, Beau was sitting in the passenger seat. And so had begun an incredible journey for the young boy.

He and Flo had criss-crossed the United States in that old rig, stopping at truck stops for greasy meals and conversations with truckers that Flo had met through the years. Beau's favorite part had been the CB, which Flo let him run for the most part. He had learned the lingo quickly,

Denim & Diamonds

and spent most of his time either listening to other truckers or talking himself. Flo was a good friend to him, and talked to him a lot. He liked that she talked to him like a real person, not like a ten year old. She told him stories about his grandparents, whom he had never met. She also told him about other relatives he had, but most of them he had never even heard of. Though Beau loved his aunt dearly, and though she talked to him a lot, she disappeared sometimes to take care of "personal business", and he had the feeling she was hiding something bad from him. Finally, one night he discovered what she had been hiding, or part of her secret, at least.

It was a dark and stormy summer night, and they were sleeping in the truck, as they often did. Beau had been curled up against the door, a blanket pulled around him. He woke up to find that Flo was gone. At first, he thought she might have just gone out to go to the bathroom, but when she didn't return, he started to worry about her. He pulled his coat on, pulled his boots on, and quietly opened the door. He slid out of the truck, landing with a light thud on the shoulder of the road. He listened intently, and peered into the darkness. It was scary out there, but he really needed to make sure Flo was okay. She took care of him, maybe he needed to take care of her this time. He drew himself up to stand as straight as he could, and took a few steps off the road. He stopped to listen again, and this time heard voices.

Slowly, carefully, he had moved towards the voices, which were coming from the trees just ahead. He had crept forward, moving from tree to tree, getting closer to the sounds. It sounded like they were several people, mostly women from the sound of it, their voices melting together in a strange chanting song. The young boy had dropped to his knees, crawling as he neared the crest of a hill. There was an orange glow, like a sunset, just over the hill. But it was too late for sunset, and too early for sunrise. He was getting chilled, but he continued to crawl the last few feet, the dampness seeping through everything, making his jeans cling to his skin. He was cold, but sweating, and his shirt stuck to him under his jacket.

He reached a fallen log at the top of the hill, and slowly, carefully, pulled himself up over the rough bark so he could peer over it. He saw a sight that was burned into his memory. A group of women were singing and dancing around a large bonfire. All had wild hair, and were dressed in black. It took the young boy a few minutes to take it all in, and he gasped when he realized that next to the fire was a large, flat rock and, on top of the rock, a man and a woman were together, their legs entangled and their hands were grasping at each other's bodies, their naked bodies were glistening with sweat, writhing together in the firelight. The little boy was horrified when he recognized the woman on the rock.

Beau shook his head violently as he pulled himself back from the memory of that scene. He remembered it as if it were just yesterday, and the memory renewed his anger at the woman who was now sleeping in the bedroom next to his. He knew it wasn't fair to be angry with her, but that didn't change the fact that he was.

Denim & Diamonds

CHAPTER NINE

The next morning, Flo added an interesting dimension to the breakfast table discussion. Joe and Rusty asked her lots of questions about her truck, her lifestyle, and the sights she had seen while on the road. She asked her own share of questions, about the ranch, the livestock and the surrounding ranches. With each question, Beau stuffed a mouthful of pancakes into his mouth, and his nostrils flared.

"Your neighbors raise cows, you say?"

"Charlotte, how 'bout another round of coffee?" Beau said, cutting Rusty off before he could answer. He caught the look Flo shot him, but he ignored it. He knew what she was getting at, and he wanted no part in encouraging her.

"Now, is that neighbors on both sides?" she persisted with her questions.

"Yup, but Jackson Brown, to our north, has the nicest herd. He takes it more seriously than Junior Rutledge, to our south. Jackson's got registered polled Herefords. Nice bunch of animals. Good beef producers." Rusty said, obviously glad to be able to contribute something to the conversation besides questions of his own.

Beau picked up his plate and carried it to the counter, clanking his fork loudly as he did, signaling the end of the meal. Rusty and Joe followed suit, nodding to

61

the women as they left. Beth offered to help Charlotte clean up, but the offer was refused. Flo stayed instead, insisting on earning her keep.

Beth followed the men to the barn, and waited until Joe and Rusty had headed out to do their chores, anxious for an opportunity to talk to Beau. She watched as he grabbed a halter from a hook and slid the door open on a two-year old's stall. He spoke softly to the animal, running his hands and eyes over every inch of him before slipping the halter over his head. As they walked down the aisle towards the arena, Beau's movements loosened up and relaxed.

"Your Aunt Flo seems very nice," Beth ventured.

"I suppose she does."

Hmmmm, she thought, *he's avoiding a direct answer*. "It's too bad you aren't as close as you used to be. I suppose that happens though. Kind of like me and my father."

He snorted, "Don't compare the two."

"I just mean that you don't seem close. My father and I weren't close either."

"Your father was a wonderful man, a hard worker who was well thought of."

"And Flo isn't?" She was getting a very strange vibe from him, and was bound and determined to get to the bottom of it. After all, what affected Beau affected the ranch, and what affected the ranch, affected her. Right?

"That's not what I mean." He started the horse moving in larger circles, and clucked softly. "And if you know what's good for you, you'll drop that subject right now."

It made Beth angry that he wouldn't talk. Just like a man to not talk about what was going on. Just like her father wouldn't talk to her mother when things started, well, whatever they started doing. And just like Bob, who wouldn't talk about the video tape of him and that slut. She closed her eyes and squeezed them tight at that memory.

Denim & Diamonds

She had been working late at home that morning, working on an S-corp election for a client, but decided to run into the office and take care of a few things. There was laughter coming from the break room, which usually signaled a birthday party. So, she went down the hallway and stood in the doorway with a smile on her face. It faded when her eyes settled on the little 19" TV screen that usually was tuned to the soaps. It was not a soap. It was a grainy video of her fiance and the firm's receptionist, on the beautiful, inlaid mahogany conference room table. She swallowed hard, and the laughter stilled when they realized she was there. In the sudden quiet, the lustful grunts coming from the television seemed amplified, and the room closed in on her.

"Hey!" Beau's shout drew her back to the dirt arena. "Are you going to answer me, or not?"

"I'm sorry. I was thinking."

"You women are always thinking. That's half your problem."

"And what is that supposed to mean?"

Beau moved the young horse into a steady trot. "Nothing. Forget it. Is there anything else you need me to do to get ready for the big barbecue?"

"Rusty and Joe are doing all the yardwork, right?" She climbed onto the top rail of the fence and balanced carefully.

"Not too keen on it, but they'll do it. I had Katie paint the fence along the driveway. That looks good."

"Will Flo be joining us for the barbecue?"

"Don't know if she can stick around or not." He pushed the horse harder, and moved him into a canter. "I'd appreciate it if you wouldn't invite her. Matter of fact, don't tell her about it."

Beth considered that for a moment, "Why not?"

"It's best for everybody if she just moves along." He shortened the lunge line, and gradually slowed the animal. His muscles rippled under his clothes, and he was graceful in every movement. It was as though he was

63

communicating every thought through the nylon lead line. It was so frustrating to be so close to a man that she found so attractive, and not be able to do anything about it. His eyes flicked to her, "And that's all I'm going to say. Just drop it."

She shrugged, "Whatever you say."

Rusty came up and leaned on the fence next to her. He nodded towards the center of the arena, "He givin' you trouble, Boss?"

That brought a smile to her face. He was giving her trouble, but not in any way she wanted to discuss with one of the ranch hands. She shook her head no, and asked him how preparations were going.

"Just fine. Joe mowed and I ran the weed whacker. Miss Charlotte made sure all the flowers there in the front are all weeded out. It looks great. We've all been workin' real hard."

It was the most words she'd ever heard him string together at once. It was usually difficult to get more than five words out of him at a sitting. They talked a few more minutes, but she had the feeling Rusty was dancing around whatever was on his mind.

"What's up, Rusty?" She decided the direct approach was best. She glanced at Beau, and wondered how the direct approach would work with him. For a moment, she considered just telling him how she felt. Or just kissing him. Maybe she could just reach up and kiss him when he led the horse through the gate.

"I hate asking, but I don't know what else to do."

"I'm sorry, I was watching the horse," she lied, hoping it was a believable lie. "What were you saying?"

"You know that old gray Chevy pickup I got? The shortbed? Well, the transmission's shot. And I ain't got the money."

"And you want me to give you the money?" Beth noticed that Beau was watching her and Rusty instead of the horse, now walking lazily around, his muzzle nearly touching the ground.

64

Rusty rubbed the toe of his cowboy boot against a fence post. "'Course not, ma'am. Not just give me. I'd pay you back, or work it off. Whatever you want, ma'am."

"Come up to the house with me and I'll get you a check. On one condition."

The two of them turned away from the arena and began walking down the aisle towards the bright sunlight. The cowhand's adam's apple bobbed up and down as he swallowed, "Anything, ma'am."

"Stop calling me ma'am, Rusty."

The next day, Beth stood at the corner of the deck, looking out over the stone patio. Beau was manning the large barrel grill. She had to smile at the get-up he had on – his apron boldly proclaimed "Caution – Man Cooking" and he had a white chef's hat perched on top of his cowboy hat. Katie was in charge of turning the crank on the ice cream machine. Charlotte was making the rounds with a large tray of beer, and it seemed as though everyone in town had turned out for the big barbecue bash. It had been Beth's idea to have a barbecue to celebrate Labor Day, and to show off their stock.

As she had hoped, many of the rodeo cowboys they had invited had indeed taken on their invitation and were now standing around chatting and admiring the horses in the back pasture. And also, as she had hoped, many of the townspeople had come, which she hoped would improve her standing in the small community. Even though she had come to think of Domino Ranch as home over the last couple of months, she knew that most of the townspeople, and even some of the ranch hands, regarded her with suspicion and considered her an outsider.

Beth was watching Beau, and couldn't help but think that he looked incredibly attractive as a cowboy chef. He was smiling and laughing, expertly flipping the hamburgers on the grill and serving up brats. Then his eyes narrowed and his face darkened. Beth followed his gaze and saw Aunt Flo coming around the corner of the house. She was dressed in her usual manner – the red tennis shoes peeked out from under a multi-colored, tie-dyed skirt, and the ensemble was topped off with a white peasant blouse accented with giant daisies. She was grinning widely, and immediately latched onto Jack Brooks, who owned the local Chevrolet dealership. Jack was smiling politely, but it was clear that he was trying to escape the conversation. Flo had taken hold of his arm, and was steering him through the crowd.

From her vantage point, Beth had a clear view of Beau, and his anger was palpable as he watched his aunt move through the crowd with Jack. Beau whipped off his apron, threw the chef's hat on the table, and stalked through the crowd, intercepting his aunt and Jack at the edge of the patio. He looked angry, she looked wide-eyed and innocent, and Jack moved away quickly, looking relieved.

Beth hadn't been able to put her finger on it, but something about him had been different since his aunt had shown up. He insisted that she would only be staying a short time, but Flo seemed to have no intentions of leaving. Beth had happened upon them several times and had the distinct impression that she had interrupted something. One of the really odd things was that Frank, who was a very friendly dog, was always on edge around the flamboyant Flo. At first, Beth had attributed it to the fact that she was a stranger. But it had been nearly a week now since she had arrived, and Frank still growled whenever she approached.

Beth felt a nudge against her right leg and looked down to find Frank, his black and white tail wagging happily. He gave a muffled woof, and she bent down to pet his silky fur. She'd never been around dogs before, and had found herself really enjoying Frank's company. Beau was fond of reminding her that Border Collies were known for their intelligence, and she had to admit that the dog seemed to understand his master's commands. As she scratched Frank's head, he looked up and she realized he had a bone in his mouth.

"Yuck, Frank! What have you drug up here now?" she asked the dog as she pulled the bone from his mouth.

The dog woofed happily, proud to present her with his find. She looked at the bone, her eyes opened wide, and she dropped it. She stared at it for a moment, and looked around to see if anyone else was looking at her. She bent down and took a closer look. It looked like a human leg bone. Not that she'd ever seen one in person, but it sure looked like the bones she'd seen on television and in the movies.

"Frank, where on earth did you get this?" she asked the dog, half expecting the Border Collie to answer her. She used her foot to kick the bone under the bench beside the house, desperately hoping that no one would see it. She was pretty sure nothing could ruin a barbecue quicker than a dug up skeleton.

"Come on, Frank, let's go get your master. Maybe he'll know what to do." she sighed and headed through the crowd, aiming for Beau. She found him, holding onto Flo's arm and speaking firmly to her.

"You promised!" he was saying angrily. As usual, the older woman was grinning widely, her gray-green eyes wide and innocent.

"I'm sorry to interrupt," Beth said, touching him on the shoulder.

He spun around to face her, frowning deeply, "What?"

"I need to talk to you. Privately," Beth said softly. Frank whined at her side.

"You, don't do anything – and you know *exactly* what I'm talking about," Beau said firmly to Flo. He sighed heavily and took Beth by the arm. He pulled her to the edge of the patio. Again, he hissed, "What?"

"There's something I need you to look at," Beth said.

"I really don't have time for show and tell," Beau said, his voice weary.

"Frank brought me a bone," Beth paused, then stood on tiptoe to whisper in his ear, "A *human* bone."

"Are you sure?" Beau asked, one eyebrow lifted. He glanced back at his aunt.

"No, I'm not. That's why I want you to come and look at it."

"Oh, good grief! This is ridiculous, Boss. Frank is forever dragging up parts of dead animals. It's probably from a deer."

The two argued back and forth for a few more minutes, but he finally agreed to go look at the bone to satisfy his boss. They made their way through the crowd, stopping to chat a couple of times. He introduced her as the new owner of Domino Ranch to a few of the rodeo cowboys, but they finally made it back up to the deck where Beth had left the bone.

Beau picked the bone up and examined it. His face darkened perceptibly, his eyes narrowed and his lips pressed together. His eyes darted over the crowd, and he took a deep breath.

"I'm no expert, but this does looks human." Beau turned to his dog, "Where'd you get this, boy?"

The dog tipped his head to the side, one ear flopped over, and whined.

Beth's mind was racing. Her hands were shaking. A human bone. That meant the rest of the body had to be around somewhere. And Frank never left the ranch, so that meant there was a body on the ranch. On her ranch. A dead body.

"We've got to get the authorities out here. I'll go see if I can find the Sheriff," she said, her voice trembling.

"No!" Beau said quickly, "You'll do no such thing. Do you know what that kind of publicity would do to this ranch?"

"Publicity? You're worried about publicity? Frank just brought us a *human* bone, for Pete's sake. Where's the rest of the body? And whose body is it?" Her voice was rising, and she could feel tears welling up and threatening to spill over.

Denim & Diamonds

He grasped her arms, and gave her a small shake, "Look at me. Let me handle this. I will deal with this. I need you to keep a hold of yourself. You just don't understand what's at stake here."

"Of course I understand what's at stake. Someone's dead," Beth said with a sneer.

"Calm down. You don't know how old this bone is. It could be an old Indian bone, for all we know. I am not going to have my ranch ruined because of some stupid bone that a dog dug up somewhere," he said firmly, his eyes drilling into her. "Now, we're going to go out there and join in the fun. It is almost time for the demonstration to start. We're going to go mingle and enjoy the show. I will deal with this myself, after everyone goes home. Understand?"

She nodded slowly and pulled away from him. Maybe he was right. She'd heard about Indian burial grounds being dug up years later, like when somebody decides to build a new golf course or housing development. That sort of made sense to her. But Beau – something about him wasn't making sense. What was going on with him? There was something about him, something dark, that scared her sometimes. He disappeared inside with the bone, and returned moments later. Beth went down the steps to the patio, but stood to the side, arms crossed.

She watched him as he returned to the barbecue grill. He was smiling and laughing, as if nothing had happened. She looked around at the rodeo cowboys that she had worked so hard to get to the ranch. She thought about all her father had worked for, how hard he had worked to build up the reputation of Domino Ranch. Maybe Beau was right, maybe she should just keep quiet for now and let him deal with it. Besides, there was something kind of romantic about just letting him take care of things.

"You must be Beth Pickard?" Beth turned to find an attractive, older man smiling down at her. "I'm Johnson Vanderengelholden. But my friends call me Van."

Her eyes opened wide, and she stammered, "Sheriff Vanderengelholden?"

"At your service. But don't hold that against me, ma'am." He touched the brim of his white felt hat and smiled as he tipped his head down. He gestured towards the round pen, "It looks like the show is getting ready to start. Shall we?"

She nodded, wondering if perhaps this was a sign, running into the Sheriff. Maybe fate was trying to tell her to tell him . . .

"I see you've met the new boss lady, Van." She turned to see Beau coming through the crowd towards them. He handed Van a beer and asked, "Is she going to show you around?"

"We were going to go watch the cutting horse demonstration over in the round pen. Want to join us?" Van answered. Beth just stood there looking back and forth from her ranch foreman to the Sheriff, still unable to find any words.

"Sure, I'll walk over with you two." Beau took Beth by the elbow and stepped between her and the Sheriff as they walked. He shot her a look that was unmistakable - she'd better keep her mouth shut or else.

The three took their seats on the hay bales that had been set up around the pen as makeshift bleachers. Beau gave her shoulder a squeeze as she sat down. Just then, Joe hollered for Beau from the chutes. He turned and gave her a long look before he turned to head for the chute.

"Is everything all right, Ms. Pickard?" Van asked.

"Oh, yes. Just so many things to keep track of today," Beth answered, and laughed nervously. She ran her hands through her hair, trying to tuck the stray strands back into the loose ponytail. "I guess we're both anxious to make sure everything goes well."

"I suppose a lot is riding on today, no pun intended." Van looked at Beth and frowned slightly. "You know, you have your father's eyes."

Denim & Diamonds

Beth tilted her head and looked up at the Sheriff. "Were you and my father friends?"

"I was proud to call your father my friend. Please accept my condolences. I know they're late, but I've been tied up with some police business for the past few months."

"I understand," Beth said, nodding.

"I wish I could have gone to the funeral, but I just wasn't able to get away. Then, quite frankly, I felt funny about showing up here and giving you my condolences when I'd never met you before." Van focused on the gray horse that was cutting a calf out of the small herd in the pen. He cleared his throat, "Rumor has it that your father gave you this place with some stipulations. Honestly, I was surprised he didn't leave the place to Charlotte."

Beth frowned and turned to look at the Sheriff. "Really? Charlotte? Why would he leave the ranch to his housekeeper?"

Van looked at her for a moment and seemed to consider whether or not to say anything more, but finally said, "You don't know about your father and Charlotte?"

She raised her eyebrows, as what he was saying started to sink in. "Know what about them?"

"Maybe I shouldn't say anything. It really should be up to Charlotte to tell you. It's for her to say, not me." Van shook his head, "I really should learn to keep my big mouth shut."

"No, no, I'm glad you said something," she said, her eyes watching the gray horse dodge from side to side, "I just feel stupid that I didn't know. Charlotte must think I'm a total idiot."

"I'm sorry," Van said, "I thought you knew."

"Unfortunately, there's a lot about my father I didn't know. I guess that's why I feel so strongly about making a go of the ranch. This is my only real connection to him. I guess I feel close to him when I'm here." She shrugged a little.

Van reached over and patted Beth's knee. The two watched the rest of the cutting horse demonstration in a

71

companionable silence. Beau watched them closely from his vantage point on the top rail of the chute. He didn't think she'd say anything about the bone, but he didn't know that for sure. She just didn't have quite the same sense of wanting to protect the ranch as he did. Besides, she didn't know the whole story. And if he had any say in the matter, it would stay that way.

He had worked to hard to create this life for himself, and now, for the first time, he was finding himself truly attracted to a woman he could imagine himself building a life with. But he would have to keep certain things from her, and he wasn't sure he would be able to have a serious relationship – a future – with someone who didn't know the whole truth about him. That was one of the reasons he had never allowed himself to get too close to anyone before. He searched the crowd for Aunt Flo, and was relieved to see her sitting by herself on a hay bale, watching the demonstration.

Denim & Diamonds

CHAPTER TEN

Beth found herself wandering around the big house all by her lonesome. After the excitement of yesterday's big barbecue, it seemed especially quiet. The clean up had been finished by noon, and now it was back to normal. Except for that pesky bone that Frank had found, that is. Everyone else had things to do. Beau and the other ranch hands, Joe and Rusty, had said they were going out to check fence. Charlotte had said she was going to town after groceries. She had offered to take Beth, but Beth felt like she would just be in the way. And honestly, she was looking forward to a little time to just explore. After all, if she had to spend the next year knocking around this ranch, she might as well get used to it. And she had to get her mind off of that bone.

She went into the living room and looked out the big picture window. Charlotte was heading down the driveway in her black Suburban. Beth couldn't help but smile, wondering if Charlotte realized that in the city a lot of people joked about drug dealers driving black Suburbans.

She turned and took a good look around. She couldn't recall ever actually being inside a log cabin until this one, but she liked the exposed log walls and the rough beam ceilings. It added a certain rustic feel to the place. It felt like a ranch house. The rough look continued with the hardwood floors that were covered with hand braided, multicolored rugs. Many of them looked like they were

73

native American designs. Beth suspected that the larger of the two recliners, which was a well-worn brown leather, had been her father's. The other worn recliner was a sage green, and was where Charlotte always sat. The recliner flanked the big sectional that she preferred. All the seating was arranged to face the stone fireplace. Tucked in an antique-looking armoire was the only nod to anything electronic, a flat screen television and DVD player. Beth suspected that her father and Charlotte, and probably Beau, had spent a lot of evenings sitting together in this room, watching movies, eating popcorn, and drinking hot cocoa.

There was a drawer under the armoir that was filled with movies, and Beth spent a few minutes perusing the titles, trying to get a glimpse into her father's life. She was surprised to find a wide variety of movies, everything from fairly recent classic chick-flicks like When Harry Met Sally, Sleepless in Seattle and You've Got Mail (she smiled as she wondered if her father had a thing for Meg Ryan), and older classics like Casanova and several Alfred Hitchcock movies.

She paused in the doorway to her father's library. Charlotte had told her this was her father's favorite room in the house, though she suspected that he probably spent most of his time outside. What little she remembered of her father seemed to fit with this room. She sighed and looked down the hallway, thinking it was probably time that she take a look at the master bedroom and think about moving into it. The guest bedroom was very nice, but it was small and a little too pink for her taste.

Although Charlotte had tried to convince Beth to move into the master suite the morning after she arrived, she had put it off. Though she didn't want to admit it to Charlotte, she hadn't really decided yet if she was going to stay. A million dollars was a lot of incentive, but not enough to make it a sure thing in her mind. Being an accountant, she had immediately run through the figures in her mind and, quite honestly, a million dollars just wasn't worth what it once was. And taking her father's challenge

Denim & Diamonds

to run the ranch for a year required her to put her own life on hold. Although her life wasn't perfect, it was still a tough decision. She was moving up quickly in her accounting firm, and was fairly confident that she would make partner in the next five years. The partners had been very generous in allowing her a year's sabbatical.

She was particularly proud of the fact that she owned her condo, which was in a very good neighborhood in Shawnee Mission, unlike so many of her friends who still rented. The condo had been her present to herself for her 28th birthday. Beth frowned as she made a mental note to call Karen, Bob's sister. She had indicated an interest in leasing the condo for the coming year in the unlikely event (in Bob's opinion, anyway) that she chose to move to the ranch for the year.

She stood at the door to the master suite, her hand resting on the cool metal of the antique brass doorknob. She took a deep breath and opened the door. She gasped, unable to believe that she would find such a rustic room so incredibly warm and inviting. It was nothing like her bedroom in her condo, which she had so painstakingly decorated in soothing shades of blue. This was natural, and comforting. The room was dominated by a king sized bed that looked as though it was made from logs. It was covered with a red flannel comforter, which was topped with several leather and faux fur throw pillows.

Meow. The little calico cat brushed past Beth's legs and hopped up on the padded window seat in the bay window. The cushions were made from a cow-print that matched the overstuffed chair that filled the sitting area by the big bay window. The reading table next to the chair had several shelves, filled with various magazines and books. An ashtray and small humidor sat on top of the table and, for a moment, Beth could almost picture her father puffing on a cigar while he reading the latest issue of *Western Horseman.* The cat looked at Beth, then calmly began grooming herself, paying careful attention to her whiskers.

Elle Robb

The stone fireplace looked as though it had been used often. The oak mantle was rough-looking, and was topped with pictures of various sizes, all featuring Quarter horses and Border Collies. One of the photos was larger than the others, and was placed in the center, and featured Beth's father and Charlotte dressed in their Western best, sitting on a matched pair of horses. It looked like it had been taken at a parade, and Beth thought she recognized the town square in Moscow.

The little cat started digging furiously at the cushion, her claws pulling at the edge and lifting it slightly. Beth moved to scold the cat, but when she tried to straighten the cushion, she felt a hinge. The cat hopped to the next cushion and blinked knowingly at her. She looked back at the cat and raised her eyebrows. She pulled the cushion up and tugged gently on the little knob that had been hidden under the cushion. A small storage space was exposed, and she dropped to her knees to look through her find. There was a leather bound scrapbook, a bundle of unopened envelopes bound together with a strip of brown cloth, and an old boot box. Ever so gently, she picked up the bundle of envelopes and sat back hard on her heels when she read her own name and her old address neatly lettered on the top envelope. It was yellowed with age, and she recognized her mother's elegant handwriting indicating "return to sender" next to Beth's crossed out name. She carefully untied the cloth strip and flipped through the envelopes, each and every one which was addressed and marked through in exactly the same manner.

Beth looked up at the little calico, who was watching her with big eyes glowing like emeralds. The cat blinked slowly and opened her mouth in a big yawn. "I don't know how you knew this was here, but I'm glad you showed me," she whispered to the little cat.

One by one, she opened the fragile envelopes with shaking hands. She couldn't believe her eyes, and the tears streamed down her cheeks as she read her father's words. She found Christmas cards, birthday cards, Valentines, and

Denim & Diamonds

each of them contained a letter from her father to his "precious Beth" and many contained little trinkets such as bookmarks or pins. She pulled a delicate filigree heart pin from a Valentine's Day card and stood up to face herself in the mirror above the chest of drawers. She pinned the gold heart to her t-shirt.

Beth stared at the young woman with her father's green eyes looking back at her, wondering how on earth she could have let her father slip away without getting to know him, and wondering how her mother could have been so cruel as to let her grow up believing that her father wanted nothing to do with her.

"Daddy, I promise, I will make you proud of me," she whispered to her reflection. "Thanks for giving me this chance to get to know you."

Meow. The cat had jumped in the storage space and was patting the cover of the leather bound scrapbook with a snow white paw. Beth bent down and retrieved the scrapbook. She sank down in the chair with the book, tucking her feet under her and settling in to enjoy the memories – the story that her father was going to tell her through his scrapbook. For a moment, she closed her eyes and let herself feel her father – the faint scent of old leather and cigars tickled her nose, and she could almost feel the warmth of her father in the chair. She took a deep breath and flipped the pages of the book carefully, surprised to find so many pages devoted to her.

It looked as though her father had kept every newspaper clipping that contained her name, even down to the honor roll listings from junior high and the academic contests that she had attended.

"Boss? Is everything okay?" Beth looked up to see her ranch foreman leaning against the door frame. He looked every inch the cowboy, and his brow was furrowed with concern. His arms were crossed casually, but his dark eyes were darting about the room, taking in the upturned cushion, the litter of opened cards and the album in her lap.

"Yes. Everything's fine," she answered as she quickly wiped a tear from her eye and cleared her throat. "What can I do for you?"

Beau took a step into the room, dropping his hands to his sides. There was something electric about his presence, and she was suddenly aware of the fact that they were the only two in the house. And she was acutely aware of the fact that she was feeling very lonely and vulnerable at the moment. She quickly closed the album and started to rise, then dropped back into the chair, lowering her defenses.

"You knew my father well, didn't you?"

"Yes, I did," Beau said, taking another step into the room. He ducked his head and caught her gaze, "Are you sure you're okay?"

"Sit down for a second and let me show you something," she patted the chair cushion next to her and smiled sadly.

Beau sat down awkwardly, stiffly, on the arm of the chair. Beth opened up to him, and told him about how her parents had separated when she was very young, how she had thought her entire life that her father wanted nothing to do with her, and how she had grown up hating the man who had given her life and then abandoned her. It was as if her life story was pouring out of her uncontrollably, as if she had turned on a faucet full blast and she couldn't turn it off. He listened attentively as she told him how she had discovered the unopened cards and the scrapbook in the storage compartment of the window seat. As the words spilled forth, so did the tears.

"So, my life has been a lie, and now there's no way I can ever make it up to him. He's gone, and I never even got a chance to get to know him," Beth finished miserably, sniffling and sucking in air. He didn't say a word, just put his arm around her shoulders and held her while she leaned into him and sobbed uncontrollably. The two sat like that until her sobs subsided into hiccups. She pulled herself up

Denim & Diamonds

straight, suddenly embarrassed that she had lost control like that – it was so unlike her.

"You must think I'm a blubbering idiot," she said, head down, still sniffling.

"No," he said. He stood and grabbed a tissue from the nightstand. He handed it to her and whispered, "You remind me a lot of your father and he was definitely not an idiot."

"Thanks," she said, amazed that he knew exactly what to say at exactly the right time, and then blew her nose loudly.

"Anytime you need a shoulder to cry on, I'm here." He sat back down on the bed, and patted the mattress beside him, "Now, you sure you're okay?"

She stiffened for a moment and then decided it was just too hard to be tough and in control all the time. She moved to sit beside him, and leaned into him again. She closed her eyes, listening to the thud of his heart in his chest and breathing in the outdoorsy smell of him. She sighed and let herself relax in his arms. She felt him kiss the top of her head, and he told her stories about her father until her breathing evened out.

CHAPTER ELEVEN

The next morning Beth woke up in her father's bed, with a quilt thrown over her. She was alone, but the smell of Beau lingered on her skin. She'd never fallen asleep with a man before that she wasn't involved with, but it was a good feeling. He had taken care of her when she needed to be taken care of. She smiled and threw back the quilt.

Half an hour later, Beth tugged on her new cowboy boots, pulled her boot cut Wrangler jeans over the top of them and stood to admire her new look in the full-length mirror. At least she looked like someone who could ride horses. Now all she needed was a cowboy hat and she'd be set. She made a screwed up face at her reflection as she recalled her first riding experience here at the ranch. She was determined to have a better ride today. She had put it off as long as she possibly could. Just to be on the safe side, she had skipped breakfast.

Meow! The little calico wound herself around Beth's feet, then stopped to look Beth squarely in the eye.

"Miss Kitty, cross your fingers and toes that I don't toss my cookies again!" Beth whispered conspiratorily to the cat.

Beth strode down the long hallway, enjoying the way her boots sounded as she walked. Charlotte was in the kitchen, kneading a loaf of sourdough bread.

"You look like you're ready to try riding again! I'm so glad. I know you had a rough start, but you'll enjoy it once you get the hang of it." Charlotte wiped her hands on

Denim & Diamonds

her apron, leaving flour handprints on the denim fabric. "Beau is a good teacher. He's very patient."

"I hope so," Beth answered with a wry grin, "He may need all the patience he can get with a beginner like me."

Charlotte shooed her towards the door, "Run along now and ride before the sun gets up too high. And don't take it personally if Beau refers to you as a rank greenhorn. That's just his way."

She suddenly found herself outside, staring at the door that had just been closed in her face. Between Beau thinking she was a "rank greenhorn" and Charlotte shooing her out the door, she really wasn't feeling much like the boss at all today. She closed her eyes took a deep breath of the clean, country air. She smiled as she thought about how much better the air smelled here than in the city, and how quickly she was growing used to it.

"Are you coming, or are you just going to stand there and breathe all day, Boss?" Beau called from the doorway of the barn.

"Oh, chill. I'm coming, I'm coming." Beth answered, not completely cross, but a little irritated that her ranch foreman had caught her unawares.

She walked slowly and deliberately down the stone path to the barn, admiring the flat paving stones that had been laid out so carefully and the rows of bright marigolds that lined the walk. The drive was empty. Even Flo's big rig was gone. She looked up to see Beau leaning back, one foot cocked against the side of the barn. He was chewing on a piece of straw, his dark eyes nearly hidden under the brim of his straw hat. She supposed he wore his hat pulled so low to hide his face. He didn't seem like the open type. In fact, she suspected that he was hiding quite a lot beneath that cool exterior. He had made one passing reference to the bone Frank found, only to assure her that he had things under control and that he would report to her whenever the situation was resolved. She wasn't exactly clear on how you could "resolve" a dead body situation, but she wasn't going to let it rest. She had laid awake thinking about it, and thought Van would deal with the situation quietly, without creating publicity. As the boss, she felt it was her responsibility to deal with the situation, but she had decided not to talk about it any further with Beau. No sense in beating a dead horse. No pun intended.

"OK. I'm here and I'm ready to learn," Beth announced as she came to a stop directly in front of Beau. He looked her up and down, and the corner of his mouth twitched as he took in her unscuffed boots and brand new Wranglers.

"Charlotte must've helped you pick out them jeans," he observed.

"What's wrong with these jeans?" she demanded, cocking one hand on a hip. Her chin jutted out stubbornly, and a frown settled on her brow.

"Not a thing, so just calm yourself down," he said. The corner of his mouth twitched more, "I just can't imagine you picking out Wranglers to wear. You seem more the Calvin Klein type."

"For the record, I haven't worn Calvins since I was in high school," she answered indignantly, "And I did not come out here to discuss my fashion preferences. I came here to learn to ride. Are you still willing to teach me, or shall I ask Joe or Rusty?"

"Don't get your panties in a wad. Come on." He pushed away from the barn wall and motioned for her to follow him as he entered the barn.

"I see Flo's rig is gone. Did she leave?"

"Doubt it. Probably just running around causin' trouble in town." He shrugged and kept walking, "Then again, with Aunt Flo, you just never know. When she decides it's time to leave, she'll just up and leave."

"I know this is none of my business, but is everything okay between you two?"

"You're right. It's none of your business."

She shrugged. He clearly didn't want to talk about it.

Denim & Diamonds

As they started down the north aisle, the little calico cat darted past them. She jumped on top of a tack trunk, then onto a stall wall and up to the hay loft. From that lofty vantage point, she trotted along above the pair of humans. She stopped occasionally to peer down at them, as if making sure they were still following her. Beth caught herself smiling at the cat's antics.

"Where'd you get that cat anyway?" Beau asked as they walked.

"What do you mean where did I get her? She was perched on the front porch of the main house the morning after I arrived here."

"Hmmm. That's funny," Beau observed. "I don't recall ever seeing that cat until you got here. I thought you brought her with you."

The two walked the next few feet in silence, then Beau stopped at the end stall, which belonged to Dingo. Beth closed her eyes and groaned.

"I know what you're thinking, but Dingo is the best beginner's horse we got. He's a sweetheart and he'll train you right. Trust me on this." Beau grabbed a black nylon halter from the horse head hook and slid the stall door open. In short order, he slipped the halter over the horse's head, led him out and hooked him to the tie attached to the wall. He pointed to the tack trunk against the wall.

"Open that up and find the curry brush. You remember what that is, right?"

Beth silently opened the wooden trunk and quickly produced a round, black, rubber brush with a red handstrap across the back. She turned to Beau and held up the brush.

"Yup," he said, nodding his head and smiling. "Do you remember what to do with it?"

"I think I do. Like this?" She approached the horse on his left side and gingerly began moving the brush in small, round strokes over the horse's neck. The horse nickered and nodded his head. She jumped back, her eyes opened wide. Beau laughed, and she frowned at him.

83

"You were doing it right. He's just telling you that it feels good and he wants you to put some muscle in it. Horses are big animals with thick skin. When you rub real gentle, you feel like a fly tickling him. So you've got to rub hard so it feels like a good back rub."

"Oh," she said. She rubbed the curry over the horse and he nickered and nodded his head again. This time she kept going, and moved down his neck and over his shoulder. By that point, she realized that he really was enjoying it. He even leaned against her, into the rubbing motion. She put her left hand against the horse's rump as she moved to the horse's right side. Beau nodded his approval as she did so.

After she finished currying the horse, she turned to Beau and lifted her eyebrows expectantly. "Now what, cowboy?"

Beau nodded towards the tack trunk and told Beth to find the all-purpose, general brush. She looked through the trunk and chose a wooden handled brush with coarse, red bristles. It also had a strap over the back. She held it up for Beau's inspection and he again nodded his approval.

As she had before, Beth started on the horse's left, at his neck, and worked her way back. Beau commented that she followed the hair's natural growth, which was something that you usually had to tell a greenhorn. When she finished the left side, she again put her hand on the horse's rump before she walked around him. When she was finished, Beau directed her to find the finishing brush. She started on the left, worked her way around, and she put her hand on the horse's rump when she switched to his left. Beau didn't have to tell her to brush the horse's face with the finishing brush. She did it on her own, pushing the horse's heavy forelock to the side so she could get his whole face. When she brushed, the horse lowered his head and gently butted against her chest. Beth laughed, and Beau actually cracked a smile.

Denim & Diamonds

"I do believe that Dingo is telling you he likes you," he observed. "Now you need to get the comb and comb out his mane and tail."

Beth did as she was instructed, until the horse's black mane and tail were tangle free and glistening. She stood back and admired her handiwork.

"He really is a beautiful horse," she said with a smile. Her head was tilted to one side, and her green eyes were shining with pride.

"He is. Horses are beautiful animals," Beau said softly. He pulled his hat down lower, but she thought she detected a flicker of interest in them.

"They really are. I can see why people love them."

He cleared his throat and said, "You're through with the easy part. Now, do you remember how to clean his hooves?"

"No, I'm sorry. I guess I wasn't paying attention the other day." Beth's face flushed – there was little she hated more than admitting that she didn't know something.

"Then you'd best pay attention today, Boss." Beau said gruffly. He talked as he worked, explaining what he was doing and, more importantly, why he was doing it. In short order, had cleaned both the front and back hooves on Dingo's left side. He handed the hoof pick to her and said, "Your turn."

She completed the task without incident, thankful that Dingo was so obliging and picked his feet up easily and without incident. When she finished, she patted the horse on the shoulder and whispered to him.

"What was that you said?" Beau asked. He put his hand to his ear like an old person would, which made her smile.

"Wasn't talking to you. I was talking to Dingo." She turned around and planted a kiss on the horse's nose. The horse stretched out his neck and curled his lip up, showing his teeth and looking a lot like Mr. Ed. Beau was unable to keep from laughing, and a large grin spread across his face. Suddenly, his smile froze and he looked

85

stiff and uncomfortable. He walked swiftly across the aisle to the small tack room and grabbed Dingo's saddle and bridle. While she watched closely, he saddled up the horse and slipped the bridle over his head.

"Dingo's ready now. Unclip the lead rope, grab the reins and let's head for the arena," Beau said. He turned and walked off, and she was left to follow with the gelding that she was beginning to think of as her own. Beau opened the gate, let her lead the horse through, and closed the gate with a clank. She stood there, wondering what to do next and feeling very inadequate, while he walked over to the far wall and flipped a switch. Dingo's ears swiveled forward as Frank Sinatra began crooning over the loudspeaker.

"Sinatra fan, huh?" she asked, a smile dancing on her lips.

"Not me. The horse," Beau answered, nodding towards Dingo, who did most definitely appear to be enjoying the sounds emanating from the speakers on each corner of the small arena. He took hold of the bridle, his hand brushing against hers. She was acutely aware of how close they were standing.

Beau seemed aware of how close they were, too. He sniffed, and she was glad she had chosen a light, floral lotion this morning. And glad she'd remembered to put on deodorant!

"Now, mount up like I showed you the other day."

Beth took a couple of hops, but managed to get up and swing her leg over in a fairly smooth motion. Beau showed her how to hold the reins properly, then took hold of her left leg to position it properly. His fingers lingered on her legs a moment too long. She had been doing yoga for years, and knew her legs were firm and well-muscled, and that her jeans fit her like a glove. She looked down at him as he walked away, looking at the faded denim molded to his body. Apparently, doing ranch work was as good a workout as any gym.

Denim & Diamonds

He stood in the center of the small arena, and had her move Dingo at a walk clockwise around the outer edge. The horse's hooves kicked up tiny clouds of dust with each step. Beth's body was fluid, moving with each step of the horse. It felt good. It felt natural, her left hand resting on her thigh, her right hand holding the reins just in front of her belt buckle, her heels down.

"You're doing fine. Now squeeze your legs together," *Oh, what a mental image that inspired!* "You're going to take him into a trot now. I want you to think of yourself as a sack of potatoes. Just let him get into a soft jog. You'll feel the rhythm. Just go with it."

Beth squeezed and found herself being bounced around the arena, feeling like her insides were being jiggled to pieces. *Sack of potatoes, sack of potatoes.* She loosened her legs slightly, and the horse slowed just a touch, and settled into a smooth, slow trot. She found herself bouncing in time to his movements, and it was like dancing – he was leading and she was following. She caught herself singing along with Old Blue Eyes and enjoying the motion, the energy of riding.

"You're doing great. Squeeze your legs just a little more and move him into a canter."

"A what?" Beth asked with a frown.

"Like running, but slower," Beau answered.

"I don't want to run." Beth said. Her voice started to tremble, and she wiped her hand hastily on her jeans.

"You can do it. Just one time around, then pull back slightly on the reins and he'll slow back down. This is Dingo we're talking about here. He's not going to go any faster than he absolutely has to. Hold onto the saddle horn with your left hand and raise up slightly in your seat, if it makes you feel better. Just slightly, though. Your butt should barely be connecting with the seat."

Slowly, carefully, and ever so slightly, Beth squeezed her knees together. The gelding's ears swiveled back and then forward again, and he began to canter. His movements were smooth, much to her surprise, and he had a rocking motion that was almost soothing. A grin split her face, and her heart filled with delight. This was a feeling like she'd never felt before. The wind blew her hair back, and she could feel the horse's muscles working under her. She felt free.

"OK. Ease up and pull back a little." Beau urged from the center. She stole a glance at him and was surprised to see a big smile on his face. His hat was pushed back and she could see that the smile had even reached his dark eyes. She turned her attention back to the horse, talking to him about how wonderful he was. Finally, she slowed him to a walk, and Beau took Beth and Dingo through some exercises, teaching her how to back the horse in a straight line and even do a rollback, which was easily the most fun thing she'd ever done.

She smiled as she thought of how proud her father would be of her, but there was a touch of sadness, too – if only she had come out here while he was alive. If only she'd taken the time, and been a little more forgiving instead of so damned bull headed.

Denim & Diamonds

<u>CHAPTER TWELVE</u>

Beau rubbed his tired, aching eyes and rolled his head from side to side. Riding the fences was a lonely job, and one that he really enjoyed. There was something about riding alone, just him and his horse. It was a mindless job – you just ride, watch the fence for things amiss and fix what needs fixing. And after spending the morning with Beth, he really wanted some time alone, some time to clear his mind.

Suddenly, he pulled Digger to a full stop. He set his jaw and gritted his teeth at the sight of the Sheriff's car in the driveway, parked right beside Aunt Flo's brightly colored semi. The last thing he wanted was the friggin' authorities sniffing around the ranch. There had damned well better be somebody hurt or dyin', he though as he urged his horse forward at a gallop toward the main house. He desperately hoped he wasn't too late to stop whatever had been set in motion.

Katie met Beau at the hitching post. She was holding one hand up, shading her eyes from the late afternoon sun, and obviously had been waiting for him. Beau pulled Digger to a sliding halt a few feet in front of Katie, swinging out of the saddle before the horse had come to a full stop.

Elle Robb

"What's goin' on?" he asked brusquely, his eyes brushing over Katie and noticing immediately that her eyes were narrowed, and her lips were pressed tightly together.

"Don't know. Nobody's telling us nothing. Sheriff pulled in here about a half hour ago. The boss lady met him and they went inside. Rusty went in to get a glass of tea and he said the boss lady and the Sheriff are sitting in the library with the door shut. He said Charlotte said something about a murder!" The words came tumbling out like rocks down a hill.

Beau frowned and tossed the reins to the girl, "I'm sure there hasn't been a murder. I'm going up to the house. Take care of Digger for me, will ya?"

"You got it," Katie answered.

Beau strode purposefully up to the house, looking more confident than he felt. He was trying to think tough, get himself geared up to face the Sheriff. He certainly wasn't feeling tough – he felt as through his world was a house of cards and a giant hand was about to flick a finger and knock one of the base cards out.

Charlotte met him at the kitchen door. Her face was drawn and tight. "They're in the library. Door's been shut the whole time. I took a tray of tea into them and heard Van say something about a murder!"

A dark storm clouded his face as he stalked down the hallway. He tossed over his shoulder, "There ain't been no murder! I'll take care of this. I'm still the damned ranch foreman around here."

He burst into the library and found his old friend and his new boss seated comfortably in the leather wingback chairs, facing the fireplace. They both turned to face him, their eyebrows raised. He paused, caught temporarily off guard with the casual feeling – they looked as though they were two old friends enjoying afternoon tea.

"Can I help you?" Beth asked politely. Van took a sip of iced tea and nodded a hello to Beau.

"I just-I mean-" Beau took a deep breath and willed his heart to stop pounding so hard, "What is going on?"

90

Denim & Diamonds

"Ms. Pickard here was telling me about that old bone that Frank dug up the other day," the Sheriff answered. He gave a little laugh, "Just between you and me, your boss is definitely a city girl. My bird dog is always dragging up something nasty. Just the other day he brought us part of a deer carcass. My wife's been on me for a week to get those bones out of the front yard!"

The three of them shared a laugh over that. Beth's face was slightly flushed. His laugh was forced, and the smile lingering on his lips never touched his eyes. He pulled the hat from his head and ran his arm across his forehead before the sweat could trickle into his eyes.

The smile faded from Van's face, "We do have a problem in these parts, though. Two of your neighbors have had cattle come up missing. You had any problems here?"

"No, sir. But I'll keep my eyes open and let you know if I hear or see anything unusual." Beau said.

"Odd that everyone around you is having problems. Think it could be one of your hands involved?"

"Oh, Sheriff, I can't believe that anyone here would have anything to do with anything illegal."

"Perhaps you just don't know them well enough to say one way or the other. Beau, how about you?"

"Van, you know these people here are like family. I know them all well. Nobody who works here would be involved in cattle rustling." Beau pulled the brim of his hat down a little further, and he shuffled his feet.

"Keep a close eye on things. Wouldn't want anything to jeopardize Ms. Pickard's chances at getting her bequest, would we?" the Sheriff's eyes narrowed, and he leaned forward, resting his arms on his knees. "Anything wrong, Beau? You got sweat just a'pouring off of you."

"I was just afraid something bad had happened here," he said awkwardly, backing towards the door. "I'd better get back to the barn and finish my chores."

"Don't be a stranger, Beau. The wife makes a pretty mean meatloaf, you know." The Sheriff smiled and sat up, then poked Beth on the knee, "Make him bring you over sometime, Ms. Pickard."

Beau glanced at Beth, who was looking up at him with those intense green eyes of hers, framed with long black lashes. Her hair was pulled back in a loose ponytail, and a stray tendril touched her right cheek. She brushed it absently back and smiled at him. Her teeth were perfectly straight, and white as new fallen snow.

"Is there anything else, Beau?" she asked, tilting her head slightly to the right.

"No. No, just wanted to let you know that I'll be leaving with Joe and Rusty for the livestock sale in Moscow as soon as they get back. Good to see you again, Van," Beau said, nodding at the Sheriff. He turned and left the room, wondering what had just happened. He suddenly felt like he was a kid again, at the mercy of those around him and unable to take control. Like he was being kept in the dark about something.

"You're frowning, Beau," Charlotte said. She was standing in the doorway to the kitchen, both hands on her hips, "That's not good. What's going on in there?"

"Can't say that I know, Miss Charlotte." Without another word, he went out the door and headed for the barn, leaving Charlotte to stand open-mouthed staring after him.

He walked quickly towards the barn, his heart still pounding. He blinked rapidly, trying to think things through. He had to think clearly, and he couldn't afford to let anything slip by him. Frank had dug up a bone, which he took to Beth. Beth called the Sheriff. The Sheriff thinks it's a deer bone, or something simple like that. So far, so good. But cattle rustling. That was a whole 'nother ballgame.

"What'd you find out, Beau?" Katie was perched on the top rung of the ladder to the hayloft.

"Nothin' to worry about. Boss got all worked up over a dead animal. Did you get Digger walked out for me?"

Denim & Diamonds

"Walked him for a bit, then unsaddled him and put him in his stall with a scoop of grain," Katie answered with a grin. She was completely comfortable with the horses, and was one of the very few people that Beau would toss his prized Digger's reins to.

"Thanks, kiddo." Beau walked down the aisle, deep in thought. He stopped in front of Digger's stall and leaned against the stall door, his face pressed against the cool metal of the bars.

"Hey, hey, Miss Katie!" Flo's high-pitched voice echoed through the barn. Beau jumped and bumped his head on the bars. He turned to face his aunt, who was wearing a wrinkled broomstick skirt in every shade of the rainbow and an orange peasant blouse.

"Katie, why don't you go check on the yearlings in the west pasture?" he called to the girl. She jumped from the ladder, landing with a thump. She saluted Beau before heading out for the pasture. Flo saluted, too, and then walked jauntily towards her nephew.

"My, my, aren't you just the mean old taskmaster today?" She asked with a sly grin.

"We need to talk," Beau said, glancing around to make sure they were alone. He didn't expect Joe and Rusty to return from checking the cattle for at least half an hour or so, and he knew Katie would do just what he had asked her to, but he was a little worried that the Sheriff and his boss would show up unexpectedly. Beth was taking her position here at the ranch way too seriously.

"What seems to be the problem, boy?" Flo asked, looking up at him with round eyes. To some, she looked innocent. To Beau, she looked fake. And it was more than just the fake eyelashes that made him feel that way. But then, he knew her better than anyone else.

"The problem is you. I want you out of here. Soon."

"That's no way to talk to your elder, boy," Flo said, with a definite edge to her voice.

"I'm not a kid anymore, Flo. I know what you are and I don't want any part of it. The people here are good. I

93

Elle Robb

have a good life here. I don't want anything to screw that up for me." Beau's voice was soft, but firm. His lips were pressed in a thin line.

"I won't screw anything up for you. Don't be silly. If anyone's going to screw anything up, it's you. You just won't accept what you are." Flo said, dismissing his concerns with a wave of her age-spotted hand.

"I am *not* like you!" Beau hissed. Flo smiled at him, a crazy, wild-looking grin. She nodded knowingly.

"You are like me. Just like your mama was. You know it and I know it. You just don't want your fancy schmancy boss lady to know what you really are." Flo kept smiling. There was a spot of her bright pink lipstick smudged on her front tooth. Beau fought the urge to wipe that wicked smile off her face.

"I am not arguing with you. I want you out. You've got until noon tomorrow." Beau turned on his heel.

"Don't you dare walk away from me," Flo said in a low voice. Her tone turned ominous, "You don't want me to tell your pretty boss lady what you really are, do you? Do you think she'd keep a thief around?"

Beau spun around and faced his aunt. "I am not asking you, I am telling you. Get out. I am *nothing* like you!"

CHAPTER FOURTEEN

Beth had enjoyed her visit with Van. He was pleasant, intelligent, and was full of information about her father. After he left, she decided to do some paperwork that she had been putting off. She was sitting in her father's library, going through the broodmare records for the ranch, when she heard a loud crash of metal against metal outside. She jumped up and ran to the window, the chair rolling back into the wall with a solid thunk.

The black and white two-horse slant trailer was still hooked to Beau's black Silverado. Beau was backing the trailer up to the round pen. Rusty and Joe were directing him as he backed. The two jumped back as the trailer rocked suddenly on its axles. There was a loud crash inside the trailer. Beau threw the truck in park and jumped out. He ran to the trailer and jumped up on the running board to see in.

Beth could feel her blood pressure rising as she watched. She spun on her heels and headed for the door. If he had dared to do what she thought he had done, after she specifically told him not to, oh, he would pay dearly!

A shrill whinny greeted her as she descended the front steps. Beau had returned to the driver's seat and was backing the trailer up to the gate. Joe and Rusty saw Beth first, and quickly ducked their heads to avoid her angry stare.

Beau had maneuvered the trailer expertly. He threw the truck in park again and jumped out, obviously anxious to get a good look at the occupant of the trailer. The sight of his angry boss stopped him short. She was standing beside the trailer, both hands on her hips, her lips pressed in a thin line and her green eyes narrowed.

"What the hell is this? Don't you dare tell me that you went and got one of those mustangs after I told you not to!" Beth's voice was high-pitched, but firm. Her chest was heaving. She was desperately trying to keep hold of her emotions.

"This stallion was well worth the money. He'll add stamina and agility to our bloodlines," he said slowly and deliberately, as though he were talking to a child.

"I told you that this ranch did not need an unpapered horse. Our horses are as close to pure AQHA as they can get. My father only occasionally allowed an unregistered horse onto the property. He would roll over in his grave if he knew you were even considering using a wild horse in the breeding program." Her nostrils flared as she talked. Rusty and Joe had backed up against the fence, trying to sink into the background so they wouldn't be noticed. It didn't work. Beth spun to face them, "And you two know that! How could you let him do this? Why didn't you call me?"

Beau was the first to respond, "Your father knew good horseflesh when he saw it. He would have seen the potential in this animal. He--"

"Don't you dare! I am the boss around here, whether you want to accept it or not! That animal will not be a part of Domino Ranch!" Beth yelled, her anger bubbling over like a volcano. How dare he ignore her! The cat stood beside her, fur standing on end.

"Like it or not, this horse will be a part of Domino Ranch. You don't want to pay for him with ranch money, fine! Suit yourself! I'll pay for him myself," he threw back at her, his anger rising to match hers.

Denim & Diamonds

"You most certainly will. And whether he is allowed to stay here at Domino Ranch is yet to be seen," she said in an ominous tone. The cat at her feet hissed. She turned on her heel and headed back to the main house, the cat following closely.

The three men stood silently, watching their boss stride angrily towards the house. The horse kicked the side of the trailer, indicating his own anger at being contained in such a confining space. The three men went into action, sliding the latch open on the trailer and letting the door swing open. They stood clear as the fiery red stallion leapt from the trailer, his hooves never touching the ramp. He galloped around the pen, his mane and tail flowing freely, his head held high like the king that he was. The well-developed muscles rippled under his skin.

"He's incredible, isn't he, boys?" Beau broke the silence. The three of them leaned against the fence, admiring the wild horse prancing in front of them.

"Yup," Rusty answered slowly, "But I do believe you done pissed the boss lady off bringing him home."

Beau nodded slowly. He ran his tongue over his dry lips, considering the situation he was in. "I'd have to say you're right about that."

"What if she makes you get rid of him?" Joe asked quietly.

The horse came to a sliding halt in front of the men, throwing up a cloud of dust. He seemed to look right at Beau, his nostrils flaring. He tossed his head and then spun away to gallop around the pen again.

"Not gonna happen. She may own this place, but I'm still the ranch foreman. And I say he stays." Beau reached into his back pocket for his can of Skoal. He grabbed a fingerful and stuffed it in his lip.

"Thought the boss lady didn't like you usin' tobacco around the barn," Rusty observed, a smile tugging at the corners of his mouth.

"I don't smoke around the barn. And I don't use chew around the house. Seems like a fair trade to me.

Besides, she's my boss, not my wife." Beau snorted dismissively. He glanced at the house and saw the curtains in the library move slightly. The window wasn't open, so it wasn't the breeze. The boss lady was probably in there watching. Well, let her watch. Maybe it was time to give her something to watch. Beau abruptly left the two ranch hands and went into the barn, leaving them staring curiously after him. He reappeared moments later, a rope in one hand and a leather halter in the other. His mouth was set in a grim line.

"Hey, you sure this is a good idea?" Joe asked, his tone clearly indicating that *he* didn't think it was a good idea.

"If she wants a show, I'm givin' her a show," Beau mumbled as he jumped up on the fence. The stallion was watching him warily from the far side of the round pen. He swung one leg over the fence, and sat on the top rail for a moment. Before he dropped to the ground, he handed the worn leather halter to Rusty.

"Hold that 'til I tell you I'm ready for it."

Rusty took the halter and nodded grimly. He nodded towards the wild horse, "Just be careful, huh?"

Beau talked softly to the horse as he walked slowly across the pen. He set one booted foot in front of the other very carefully and deliberately. The horse watched him warily, tossing his head occasionally. His forelock was long and tangled, hanging well below his large brown eyes which were framed by the hanging locks of hair. Each time Beau got within about ten feet of the horse, the animal would rear up, flailing his hooves at the approaching stranger and then run the second he dropped to all fours again. Beau continued, patiently, continuing to talk softly to the horse the whole time. Joe and Rusty watched anxiously from the side, both worried about what would happen when the horse tired of running from the tall dark man who insisted on pestering the stallion.

Just as Beau had guessed, Beth was watching from the library window. She had pulled the chair over so she

Denim & Diamonds

could sit and watch. She was entranced by the sight of the cowboy and the wild stallion. Both were equally stubborn, and equally attractive. Each was beautiful in a wild way. She was still angry that he had brought the mustang home from the auction – Lord only knew how much he had paid for the unbroken, wild stallion.

She had to admit the horse was a fine specimen, but that didn't excuse the fact that Beau had gone directly against her wishes. What on earth would they do with a wild mustang on a working ranch? And though she would not admit it to anyone else, she was terrified of what could happen – what would happen – when Beau tried to break the horse. This wasn't like the quarter horses he was used to dealing with. This was a wild animal, unused to human contact and unwilling to please them. Even though she was afraid the man would be on the losing end of this confrontation, she just couldn't tear herself away from the window.

The stallion had stopped again and was pawing the ground nervously. He flipped his tail, obviously irritated at the whole situation. He watched warily, his head lowered, as the cowboy approached slowly. When Beau got to within about ten feet, the horse stopped pawing and stood still, his muscles quivering. He seemed to be considering the man in front of him, sizing him up. Beau inched forward, still talking in his most soothing voice. He was within an arm's length. He stretched his hand out slowly towards the horse's muzzle, his palm down. The horse's nostrils flared as he smelled the human's hand.

Suddenly, the horse let out an unearthly scream and reared up, lashing out at the man with his hooves. Beau flew backward, landing with a thud on his rear end. He hit the ground hard, and it jarred him badly. Time seemed to stand still as those deadly hooves hovered above him, then the horse spun and galloped away. Beau sat for a moment, holding his shoulder where the stallion's hoof had grazed him. Rusty and Joe jumped into action, running across the pen, screaming like banshees. The horse's eyes opened wide and he maintained the greatest distance possible between himself and the loud humans.

When they reached Beau, they helped him to his feet and steered him towards the walk-through gate, in spite of his objections. They kept glancing over their shoulders to make sure the wild stallion kept his distance. Once they were through the gate, Beau leaned heavily against the trailer. His breath was ragged and his shoulder was throbbing. He looked down to see a dark stain spreading across his cotton shirt. Blood didn't bother him as a rule, but his legs were shaking and he slid down to sit on the running board. Joe and Rusty were on either side, still holding onto him. They shared a look, and Joe shivered.

"Do you realize how close that hoof came to your head, man?" Joe whispered. He looked as though his own legs might be feeling a little like spaghetti.

Footsteps pounded on the driveway behind them and Beau looked up as Katie came around the truck, followed closely by Beth and Charlotte. The girl was the palest of the three, and her eyes were the widest, but by a narrow margin. Charlotte kicked into action.

"Joe, go get the keys to the Suburban and pull it over here. Rusty, go to the office in the barn and get the first aid kit. Katie, go get me a wet washcloth." Charlotte gently lifted the shirt away from Beau's shoulder and exposed a gash about four inches long, that looked pretty deep. Blood wasn't gushing, but it was certainly flowing. Beth leaned forward and looked, then quickly pulled back when she saw the raw, exposed flesh.

"It's just a scratch," he said, but his voice was weaker than Charlotte cared to hear.

"What's the problem?" Flo appeared out of nowhere, hovering anxiously around the edge of the group huddled around Beau. "What happened? Let me help."

Beau frowned when he heard Flo's voice and he whispered through clenched teeth, "Get her the hell out of here."

Denim & Diamonds

The small group closed in protectively around Beau, and ignored his aunt.

"What can I do?" Beth asked. Before Charlotte could answer, Joe pulled up in the Suburban, wheels sliding in the loose gravel. Katie came running from the barn with a wadded up cloth and a small white plastic case marked with a big red cross on the front. Charlotte held the back door open while Rusty helped a protesting Beau into the back seat. Beth ran around to the other side and jumped in. Beau scooted into the center, and Charlotte climbed in after him. Seconds later, Rusty slammed the front door and the four of them were pulling out of the driveway. Joe and Katie shouted a promise to keep an eye on the stallion, and Charlotte promised to call them from the hospital. Through it all, Beau continued to protest, but to no avail.

Charlotte had Beth hold Beau's shirt out of the way and she cleaned the wound as Rusty raced down the highway. Charlotte and Beth took turns keeping pressure on the wound with gauze pads from the first aid kid. The twenty minute drive to the little hospital in Moscow seemed to take forever.

The hospital was small and many of the nurses knew Beau. Beth wasn't sure if that was a good thing or a bad thing at first, but he seemed to get treatment fast enough. The trio waited anxiously in the waiting area until a well-endowed blonde nurse wheeled Beau out in a wheelchair. He was bandaged and a little pale, but was also grinning like a maniac. The pain pills had kicked in.

Once they had returned to the ranch, it was decided that Beau would stay in the main house for a few days to allow his shoulder time to heal. Joe and Rusty helped him into the house, and got him into the bed in the guest bedroom. Beau looked around at the very feminine room and frowned deeply.

"This ain't no room for a real man," he grumbled.

"Looks better than that hell hole you call a bedroom, man," Joe answered with a snort. He helped arrange the pillows to make Beau as comfortable as possible.

Charlotte appeared with a small silver bell. She sat it on the oak night stand and instructed Beau to use it any time he needed anything at all. Once she was convinced that everything had been done that could be done, she herded everyone out of the room and left him to rest. He was already groggy from the pain meds, and was snoring before Charlotte had pulled the door closed behind her.

When he awoke several hours later, it took a moment for his eyes to adjust and for him to realize that the pink room he was in was not a dream. He blinked and started to stretch, until the sudden pain in his shoulder froze him. He slowly lowered his arm, groaning as he did so.

"Hurts pretty bad, huh?"

Beau glanced over at the low-backed chair by the window. Beth was sitting there, her feet tucked under her. Her curls framed her face, and she looked as though she had been resting, too.

"A little," he said, pain straining his voice.

"It's time for more pain pills," she said. She tipped two pills out of a medicine bottle and handed them to him, then offered a glass of water. She watched silently as he took the pills and examined them. After a moment, he shrugged slightly with his good shoulder and tossed the pills in his mouth. He threw back a drink of water and handed the glass back.

"Thanks," he said gruffly. He looked his boss up and down, "Been here long?"

"Long enough to hear you snore." she caught his eyes and stared at him intently, her green eyes boring into his, "Do you realize how lucky you are? That horse could have killed you today."

"But he didn't." He broke the stare and looked around the room. "I never realized the old man had a pink room."

"Very funny." She rose to her feet and stood over her foreman, "I'm getting rid of that horse. You could have

Denim & Diamonds

been killed today. I will not have a dangerous animal like that on my ranch."

Beau lifted himself up with his good arm, "That animal is mine, not yours. You leave him right where he is. I will decide what to do with him."

She moved towards the door, her green eyes flashing, "As I said, I will not have a dangerous animal on this ranch. I am the boss around here."

He spat, "You touch that horse, and it'll be the last thing you do."

"I doubt that very much." She turned her back to him and walked across the room. "Oh, your girlfriend called. She wants you to call her when you're feeling up to it."

She stalked out the door, slamming it behind her.

CHAPTER FIFTEEN

Beth loved early morning rides. There was something so peaceful about being out when it was cool, just her and her horse. After her blow up with Beau earlier in the week, she hadn't been sleeping well and hadn't spent as much time in the barn as she had been before the mustang arrived. Just as she thought he would, he ignored the doctor's orders and returned to the light duty around the barn just a day after his injury. Charlotte intervened on his behalf and convinced Beth to let him keep the stallion. Though she didn't want to admit it, he did seem to be making progress with the mustang. Katie reported that he had the horse halter trained and was able to groom him already. For whatever reason, he was the only one that had been able to get anywhere with the animal.

Beth sighed, determined to think about something other than the differences of opinion that caused her so much angst. Getting out for some fresh air seemed to be just what the doctor ordered for her to clear her mind and gain some perspective on things. Riding allowed her to focus on something other than the ranch foreman that was testing her limits, and she thought she was doing pretty good for her first solo ride. She reached down and rubbed Dingo's neck.

Denim & Diamonds

She had grown very attached to the gelding – he seemed to sense what she wanted to do before she knew she wanted to do it. It was like power steering on horseback. This morning, Katie had pointed out the easy path that ran alongside the creek that ran through the ranch. Walker Creek was what everybody called it. The water made a soothing sound as it gurgled along through the rocks, and Beth was enjoying the muscular feel of the horse beneath her, and the creak of the leather. She closed her eyes and enjoyed the warmth of the mid-morning sun.

She smiled as she thought about how much her life had changed. Just a few short months ago, she had been a corporate dragon lady, at work early every morning and working late every night. She had lived in a concrete jungle, high stress and on the go constantly. Now her life consisted of horses, dogs, pedigrees and fencing. She sighed deeply, and took a deep breath of the fresh air, knowing in her heart that nothing smelled better than grass and horses.

Suddenly, a sound that didn't belong jerked her back to reality. She pulled Dingo to a stop and held her breath, listening as hard as she could. She heard it again. Voices. It sounded like a man and woman arguing. And it sounded like it was coming from just ahead. Beth slid off the horse and dropped the reins, silently thanking her father for demanding that every one of his horses be trained to ground tie. The voices were strained, but the speakers were trying to keep their voices down. She crept forward, straining to hear. As she got closer, she was pretty certain that she recognized Beau's voice, and that of his crazy aunt. She paused, hesitant to eavesdrop on her foreman's private conversation, but curiosity won out and she peered over a fallen tree.

Sure enough, Flo was sitting on the ground and Beau was standing over her. Beth could not make out what they were saying, but Beau appeared angry. His aunt seemed unresponsive to his anger, and seemed to be dismissing him. Beth dropped to all fours and crept forward

105

a few more feet. She looked through the branches of a bush.

"I don't believe you," Beau hissed angrily.

"Believe or don't believe. That is your choice, boy. But it's the truth. And you are destined to follow in their footsteps," Flo said evenly. She was holding something in her hand. Beth wasn't sure, but it looked like a very old book, maybe bound in leather.

"I am proud to follow in their footsteps. But they were not what you say they were! You're just a crazy old woman." Beau practically spat the final words at the old woman kneeling on the cold ground. She had laid the book on the ground, where it laid open, the pages flipping back and forth in the light autumn breeze. There was writing on the pages, and a few drawings.

"You know it's true. It is obvious when you deal with the animals. Think about your mustang stallion. He knows."

"I have a way with animals. There's nothing magical about that."

"Oh, my boy, you're wrong, it is magick. You have the power."

"No such thing. I know what you've been doing. I've heard about the cattle disappearing in these parts, and I won't have you doing that around here. If you aren't out of here by noon tomorrow, I'm going to the Sheriff."

"He's under my-"

"He is not! He's just being nice to you because he thinks you're nuts. I don't want to turn you in, but I will. And if I hear that you've done anything besides stealing, I swear to God--"

Beth's leg started to cramp, and she shifted her weight. A twig snapped under her weight and she froze. The voices were silent. She held her breath.

"Who's there?" Beau called out. She closed her eyes, silently praying that Dingo had stayed put and would not respond to him. She began slowly, very slowly, backing down the hill towards her waiting horse. Finally, she heard

Denim & Diamonds

the voices over the hill resume. When she reached Dingo, she quickly led him through the woods and out into a clearing. Once she could no longer hear the rush of the water, she decided it was safe to mount her horse. She urged him to a slow jog and headed back to the barn. She spent the rest of the ride wondering what she had happened upon by the creek.

There was no doubt in her mind that Beau had been hiding something all along. Now her curiousity had been piqued.

She frowned when the main house came into sight. She didn't recognize the red Chevy stepside that was parked in the drive. As she got closer, she noticed a tall brunette standing on the front porch talking with Charlotte. The two were laughing and talking, definitely fairly well acquainted. Beth thought the woman looked familiar, but she couldn't quite place her. Katie was waiting for her outside the barn, and was chewing angrily on a piece of beef jerky. Beth slid off the big horse and landed with a thump on the grass.

"Who's that?" Beth asked Katie. Katie scrunched up her nose and made a face.

"That's Janice. She's a bitch," Katie replied, her tone matter-of-fact and very grown-up for a 13 year old.

"You shouldn't use words like that," Beth reminded Katie, but couldn't contain her smile at the teen's description of the tall brunette.

"Well, she shouldn't be one," Katie retorted. "Beau deserves a whole lot better than a – a witch like that."

"So that's the girlfriend?" Beth nodded slowly, remembering seeing her in town that night on the square. And she had been at the barbecue, too.

"That's what she'd like, anyways. I'm not real sure Beau would consider her a girlfriend, though."

"Really? Why not?"

"I think he just uses her for sex," Katie answered, her tone serious. Beth coughed and blinked.

"Uses her for sex, huh? And how would you know that, young lady?" Beth asked sternly, trying not to smile.

"I heard them in the hayloft after the barbecue. I've heard them before. She's a screamer." Katie tilted her head to the side and looked thoughtfully towards some unknown point in the distance, "She's a moaner, too. He tells her to shut up a lot. But she still makes a lot of noise when they're doing it."

Beth felt a flush creep up her cheeks, and a smile tugged at the corners of her mouth. She bit her lower lip to keep from laughing, "I see. I think I'm going to go chat with her for a moment. Would you like to put Dingo up for me?"

"Sure!" the girl answered enthusiastically, her blonde ponytail bobbing up and down. Beth patted her horse on the shoulder and gave him an affectionate peck on the cheek before heading towards the main house. She was acutely aware of the fact that the conversation stopped cold when she approached the steps. Charlotte looked vaguely uncomfortable, and the brunette was smiling smugly, her arms crossed over her ample chest.

"Hello, Charlotte. And Janice, isn't it?" Beth asked with a gracious tone.

"Yes, how sweet of you to remember!" Janice gushed, as Charlotte mumbled something about tea and escaped into the house.

Beth pointed to the rocking chairs and suggested they sit and chat for a few minutes while they waited for Charlotte to return with the iced tea.

"So, what brings you out to the Domino?"

"Just came out to see my Beau. He just works so many hours, I don't get to see him near enough. He comes by my house fairly regular – at least three or four times a week – but that's just not enough. I just can't get enough of that man!" Janice actually batted her eyes and Beth fought the urge to puke. "So, tell me about your man. Beau tells me you've got a rich boyfriend up in the City."

Denim & Diamonds

"Oh, Bob? He's not really my boyfriend," Beth answered, her chair creaking as she rocked harder, remembering the video of Bob screwing his secretary. She had a sudden image of Beau and Janice together in the hayloft. Knocking boots seemed like an appropriate term for that mental snapshot.

She smiled sweetly at Janice and continued, "Actually, he was my fiance, but we're sort of taking a time out."

"Well, sure. Sure. I can see that, what with you being way out here and everything. I'm sure it'd be very stressful trying to plan a city wedding while you're out in the middle of nowhere," Janice said. Her eyes sort of glazed over with a dreamy look, "You know, when I was younger, I always said I was going to have a Western wedding – you know, me and the groom'd wear white cowboy boots, and white cowboy hats, and everybody'd sit on hay bales. I'd want to ride in on a white horse, sitting sidesaddle."

"That would be interesting," Beth said. She couldn't help but grimace as she thought about how Beau would look all dressed in white. He just didn't seem like an all-white kind of guy.

"I bet you were going to have an uptown city wedding. Something really elegant, right?" Janice asked, leaning forward in her rocking chair.

"My wedding dress was - is a Vera Wang. It's very sleek and sophisticated," Beth felt the bile rise in her throat when she remembered how much that dress had cost. The dress that was now hanging in a closet, covered with plastic, probably for eternity.

"Vera Wang? Isn't she an actress?" Janice asked, her brown eyes wide as a doe's.

"She's a designer. A lot of actresses wear her dresses, though."

"That's probably where I've heard the name, then. You know," Janice leaned forward and whispered conspiratorily, "I always act like the cowgirl type, but my dream is to someday run away to the City and make it big as a dancer. I been taking ballet and tap classes since I was four. My mama says dancers make a lot of money. I've heard the really good dancers, who do unusual dances, are called exotic dancers, and they can make hundreds of dollars a day."

"I see," Beth answered, nodding slowly, thinking, *or a night*. She couldn't help but wonder if Mama had any clue what she was talking about.

"But I'll give that dream up if Beau wants to stay here. We haven't really talked about it yet." Janice settled back in her chair and flipped her long, wavy hair over her shoulders. Beth sighed as she admired those waves. Her own curls were just unruly, nothing wavy about them.

The front door burst open and Charlotte appeared with a tray filled with a glass pitcher of iced tea, three glasses, a little bowl of lemon slices and a tray of sugar cookies. Charlotte's face looked slightly pinched and she looked flustered. She carefully set the tray on the wicker table sitting between the rocking chairs.

"Here we go, girls. Tea and cookies?"

"Pull up a chair, Miss Charlotte. We can serve ourselves." Beth said with a smile intended to put Charlotte at ease.

"Well, okay, then. I suppose. I hope I didn't interrupt your conversation," Charlotte said, lowering her ample frame into one of the wicker chairs.

"Of course not," Janice answered, a mouthful of cookie muffling her words, "we were just discussing our weddings."

Charlotte paused a split-second, then dropped the rest of the way into the chair. Her wide eyes focused squarely on Beth, "Really? Your weddings? Do tell, child."

"Janice here was just telling me about her Western wedding," Beth said, lowering her head slightly and shooting Charlotte a meaningful look.

"Did you know that Beth has a designer wedding dress?" Janice said breathlessly. It was obvious that she

Denim & Diamonds

was in awe of the city-girl image. "That's just so cool. I bet she has the most beautiful wedding. I bet it even gets covered in the society pages of the big city newspapers."

Charlotte raised her eyebrows and looked pointedly at Beth, "When is this wedding to take place, Miss Beth?"

"Don't worry, Miss Charlotte, there's nothing definite in the works. Of course, I'm sure you remember me telling you about the situation with Bob?" she desperately hoped Charlotte wouldn't say too much. Right now, she would just as soon that Janice not know that she was available. She wasn't really sure why, but she didn't want Janice to feel that she had any competition with respect to Beau. Not that a short, skinny redhead like her would be any competition for the tall, shapely brunette. And in a weird way, she was kind of enjoying the adoration and envy that was radiating from Janice.

Charlotte just raised her eyebrows, then took a long sip of tea and leaned back in her chair. The three women sat together, sipping their tea and watching the broodmares grazing in the front pasture. The four mares stopped in unison and looked off to the west. The three women turned to follow the horses' gaze and saw Beau riding up on Digger. He looked up and saw the group on the porch. He tipped his hat and turned Digger towards the hitching post. He took his time unsaddling the horse, carefully keeping his back to the women. Beth couldn't help but admire the way his jeans hugged his ass – She shook herself when she realized she was staring, and helped herself to another cookie.

Charlotte smiled at her, which just made Beth blush more. Charlotte turned to face Janice.

"So, Janice, you have a western style wedding planned?" Charlotte asked, her face the picture of innocence. Beth looked down, studying the crumbs on her lap.

"Well, it's what I've always dreamed of. But, nothing's certain yet. I'm sure you'll be the first to know when it happens, Miss Charlotte!" Janice said, finishing brightly. Janice stood and smoothed her hair, then bounced down the steps towards Beau. "So good to see both of you again! See you at the hayride next weekend!"

"Oh, Miss Beth, I forgot to tell you that Van stopped by early this morning. Said he'd be by for the hayride tonight and would talk to you then." Charlotte said as she stood and picked up the tray.

Beth nodded absently, and stole another glance at her foreman, meticulously arranging the tack on the hitching rack. Janice was leaning casually against the hitching post, chattering away. Katie appeared from the barn to help carry the tack into the tack room, and Beau led Digger into the barn. Janice followed at a safe distance. Beau just couldn't imagine him with someone as shallow as Janice, but maybe that was what he wanted. Someone pretty to look at, someone to jump in the sack with, someone whose hair didn't frizz out of control every time the humidity took a jump up. Beth sighed and took another cookie.

CHAPTER SIXTEEN

Beth studied her reflection in the mirror, critically turning her head this way and that. She pulled her hair back and held it there, examined her ivory skin. Thank goodness it was actually blemish free. She had lost weight since moving to the ranch, and her cheekbones were more pronounced than they had been in the spring. She let her hair down, then pulled it back up again. She nodded. Up it would be. She chose a pink velvet scrunchie and put her hair up in a half ponytail. After looking through her meager supply of makeup, she decided to add a touch of blush, some eyeliner and finished off with a quick brush of mascara over her lashes.

Once satisfied with her face, she turned around to look at her reflection in the mirrored shower door. She smiled as she realized she'd lost weight all over. Her leg muscles were more pronounced, and her stomach was flat. She turned to the side and grinned. Her butt was the tightest it had ever been!

Beth went into the large walk-in closet that she still felt lost in, and started flipping through the rack of shirts. She honestly couldn't recall ever having been on a hayride before, and she didn't have a clue what to wear. Surely it would be a casual affair. Everything here at the ranch was casual. Besides, she'd be sitting on hay! She pulled a pair of classic straight leg blue jeans from the shelf and jumped up and down as she tugged them on. After flipping through the rack again, she chose a black turtleneck that was just a little clingy. Then she slipped into a fur-lined denim vest. She headed for her bedroom, looking around for her distressed leather lacers. Once she had them on and pulled her jeans over the top of the boots, she stood and examined herself in the full-length mirror.

"Your butt looks fine," Katie said from the doorway. "Come on!"

"I wasn't looking at my butt," Beth said with a scowl.

Katie laughed, "You were, too! Come on! Everybody's out by the barn, and Miss Charlotte told me to come and get you. Shoot, even my parents are here already."

Beth smiled at the girl who acted more like a younger sister than a part-time pooper scooper. Katie grinned back, then continued, the excitement making her talk fast, "What do you like best about hayrides?"

"I haven't ever been on one."

"Oh, my gosh! I can't imagine that! My favorite part is the singing. Or maybe it's the spiced cider, or maybe-"

"Okay! I get it! You like it all – now let's get out there and get this show on the road." Beth glanced around the master suite, and smiled at the little calico curled up in the pillows before she turned off the light and shut the door.

When they stepped out the front door, she gasped in surprise. The parking lot and driveway were full of pickups and cars. A large group of people were gathered by the front door of the barn, laughing and talking. There were flickering jack-o-lanterns sitting around in strategic locations, and a couple of scarecrows were leaning against the fences, their grinning faces a little bit creepy in the twilight. Strings of orange lights had been strung around the barn and over to the round pen, creating a party atmosphere. Charlotte was in her element, making sure everyone had a cup of hot cider and mingling with all the neighbors and townspeople. Her head was bobbing up and down and her laughter carried on the evening breeze. Katie ran ahead, meeting up with two other giggling teenage girls. Those three would be trouble when they got older, Beth was quite sure.

The Sheriff was sitting on a hay bale talking to a couple of people that Beth didn't recognize. He nodded to her and raised his cup of cider in greeting as she approached. The car dealer with the slicked back hair was once again cornered by Aunt Flo. He didn't seem as anxious to get away from her as he seemed at the Labor Day barbecue. In fact, he seemed to be completely smitten with the petite woman at his side, and couldn't take his eyes off of her.

Beth steered clear of them and headed for the other side of the group, intent on mingling as much as possible in hopes of drumming up business and support for the ranch. She hadn't said anything to anyone at the ranch, but she had some business ideas that she fully intended to initiate as the new ranch owner, and it would certainly help to have some personal contacts before she opened the business.

"Beth! Beth! Over here!" Janice's voice sang out over the mumble of voices. Beth looked around for a moment, then spotted Janice standing beside the tractor that was hooked to the flat bed wagon. She was dressed in tight black low rise jeans and an off white sweater with a faux fur collar, which set off her dark hair well. She had her hair pulled back and up with a leather barrette. With the high heels on her black cowboy boots, she easily stood half a head taller than Beth.

"Glad you could make it," Beth said. Janice leaned down and gave Beth a perfunctory hug and brushed her cheek against hers.

"I haven't missed a Domino Ranch hayride in the five years they've been puttin' them on," Janice said, gesturing towards the crowd, "It's the social event of the fall season around these parts."

"Apparently so," Beth said absently. She felt a little awkward around Janice, but Janice seemed perfectly at ease with her. She had the distinct impression that the other woman was lonely and looking for a friend, but she had a hard time getting past the fact that Janice was sleeping with Beau. That irritated Beth to no end, because she knew that Beau had absolutely no interest in a city girl like her. Even if he did, he was not exactly the type of man that she imagined herself spending the rest of her life with. For goodness sakes, he was her employee! Beth looked around, realizing that she hadn't seen him yet. She hadn't seen Rusty or Joe yet, either. She frowned, wondering where the guys could be.

"Beth?" Janice poked her in the arm, causing her to jump.

"I'm sorry," Beth said, turning her attention back to Janice, "What were you saying?"

"I asked if your fiance is going to be able to join us tonight," Janice said, blinking expectantly.

"No. Bob's just so busy. He couldn't get away," Beth lied. Actually, she was embarrassed to admit that she had broken down and asked him if he'd like to come, and he had turned her down. She really was kind of lonely sometimes, even though she had been quickly accepted at the ranch. So, when he had called last week to discuss a client's tax planning with her, she had asked him to come out for the hayride. She winced as she recalled his response – laughter. Janice poked Beth, causing her to jump again. Beth looked up and Janice was staring at her.

"I was just saying that it's too bad you sent Beau to that special auction tonight," Janice said with a slight frown.

"Auction?" Beth asked, her own frown forming.

"She's talking about that special bull sale, Miss Beth," Rusty appeared at Beth's side, startling her. For once, his cowlick had been smoothed down, and his jeans and shirt looked brand new. He caught Beth's eye and

Denim & Diamonds

winked, "Remember that sale you told Beau to go to because you wanted that bull that was goin' to be sold?"

"Sure, sure. The auction," Beth said, confused, but willing to go along with Rusty for the moment. "Where's Joe?"

Rusty's smile got bigger, "Miss Beth, you must be workin' too hard. Don't you r'member, you sent Joe with Beau to help him with that bull."

"Oh, I see," Beth said, not seeing at all.

"That better be one special bull," Janice groused, "I was really lookin' forward to snuggling up with my Beau-Beau in the hay."

Beth winced as she bit her tongue. Rusty poked her in the ribs and grinned great big. He turned to Janice and said, "This is a family get-together. You and Beau don't need to be doing no hay rollin' when there's young 'uns around."

Beth listened as Janice and Rusty traded a few verbal jabs, only mildly interested in the exchange. She glanced over the crowd, surprised that she actually recognized a lot of the people. Penny Jenkins, who ran the little café in town, was chatting with Roger Andrews, who ran the local hardware store. Evelyn Richardson, the slightly eccentric woman who spent her days feeding the pigeons on the town square (and who no one was able to convince that there *were* no pigeons on the town square) was standing by herself, smiling and talking in a very animated fashion. The rather pompous Weldon B. Willingham III was rocking back and forth on his heels, explaining the value of estate planning and tax avoidance to a small group of slightly angry looking people who nodded as they listened to his sage advice.

Charlotte had warned Beth to steer clear of the distinguished Mr. Willingham, who had once been the town's most successful attorney, but had since declared himself a non-citizen and established his little lot in town as a separate country. He flew a flag which he had designed himself, and refused to pay taxes. And tried to convince other people in Moscow to follow his example and secede from the United States. Beth had been less than excited to know that the gentleman would be joining them, but Charlotte had assured her that he was a harmless old man who everyone listened to out of politeness and respect for their elders – but let it go in one ear and out the other. Still, the idea of having him here made her a little nervous. She sincerely hoped that he and Aunt Flo wouldn't find themselves alone. That could be a combustible situation.

As she looked over the crowd, a waving hand caught her eye. The Sheriff rose and started working his way through the crowd. Beth left Rusty and Janice to bicker by themselves and started working her way through the crowd, too.

"Beth, so good to see you," the Sheriff said, leaning forward to peck Beth on the cheek.

"Please, call me Beth. Glad you could make it," Beth said, meaning it.

"Wouldn't miss it for the world. Has Frank drug any bodies up the house lately?" Van asked, a smile splitting his leathered face.

"No, thank goodness. No," Beth laughed. Just having the Sheriff here made her a bit nervous, but she couldn't explain why. He seemed like a nice enough man, she supposed she should feel comforted by his presence. "Anything new going on in Moscow?"

"Just the usual. A few peace disturbances. A few of the farmers around have been complaining. Seems like we may have a mountain lion in the area, or something of the sort. Something's been bothering the stock around here. There's been a few dead cows found. And some just plain missing. That's why I stopped by here earlier. Just wanted to make sure you were keeping a close eye on your stock. Old Mr. Jameson to your west has had two heifers die on him, cut up something awful."

"That's too bad," Beth answered. She felt a shiver work its way up her spine, and she looked out into the

Denim & Diamonds

gathering dusk. "I didn't know we had mountain lions around here."

"Not a lot. But it only takes one hungry mountain lion to cause problems." Van looked at Beth, his gray eyes intent on hers. "You had any problems here?"

"No. I'm sure the boys would tell me if they had run across anything like that," Beth answered, her voice sounding much more confident than she felt.

"Haven't lost any animals?" Van asked.

"No," Beth answered again, more firmly this time.

Van looked around the crowd, his gaze settling on the bright purple poncho that enveloped Aunt Flo. "I see Beau's aunt is still around. How's that workin' out?"

"I guess you'd have to ask Beau that," Beth answered stiffly. This conversation was making her very uncomfortable. It felt more like a fishing expedition by the Sheriff than a friendly conversation. To her surprise and relief, Janice popped up behind the Sheriff.

"Sheriff! What brings you here tonight – business or pleasure?" Janice tucked her hand into the crook of the older man's arm.

"For me, there's really never a separation of business and pleasure," the Sheriff said, looking directly at Beth as he spoke. Beth felt another shiver go up her spine.

"OK, folks! Who's ready for a hayride?" Rusty was standing on the tractor, a big grin on his face. Everyone cheered and started piling onto the wagon. Beth found herself being pulled along with the crowd towards the rear of the wagon. Hands reached down and helped her up, with Janice right behind her. The two found themselves sitting together towards the back of the wagon.

Katie waved at Beth from the front of the wagon. The girl looked completely happy. The couple sitting beside Katie were obviously her parents – the woman had the same blonde hair, pulled back in a ponytail just like her daughter's, and the man had the same wide smile. Beth was glad to see that they'd made it. Katie spent so much time at the ranch, Beth had often wondered if the girl even had

119

Elle Robb

parents. Katie and her friends were flipping through a case of CD's, and had a small boom box sitting between them. Within moments, strains of the Monster Mash could be heard and everyone was singing along with the familiar words. The tractor chugged forward and the hayride was underway.

Beth and Janice chatted amicably, staying on fairly safe topics, if you can consider wedding plans safe. The Sheriff had taken a seat directly across from her, and was clearly watching her. The music continued, and the group sang along with old favorites such as Purple People Eater and Witch Doctor. She got caught up in the moment, and found herself singing along, and swaying with the music. Suddenly, the tractor and wagon jerked to a stop. All eyes turned to Rusty, who had turned to face them.

"Something's wrong with the tractor. I'm gonna take a look. Just keep singing and enjoy yourselves. I'm sure it's nothin' serious."

Beth and Janice exchanged a nervous glance. She looked over her shoulder, thinking about mountain lions and missing livestock. The moonlight washed over the field, and shadows flitted here and there. Clouds drifted through the sky, partially blocking the moon. She caught movement out of the corner of her eye and squinted into the darkness. Nothing moved. The crowd murmured, and Katie had turned the music off. An owl hooted in the distance. A twig snapped and Beth's head swivelled to the right. Again, she squinted into the darkness, straining to make out the shapes in the night.

Suddenly, Penny screamed and jumped into the center of the wagon. Her eyes were wide.

Then one of Katie's friends pointed and yelled, "There's something out there!"

Someone else screamed and everyone began moving to the center of the wagon. A shape appeared beside the tractor, a humpbacked figure with a hood over its head was moaning and groaning. Penny fainted into Roger's waiting arms. Katie reached out and pulled the mask from the figure, revealing Joe's grinning face. He jumped at Katie and yelled, "Boo!"

Everyone laughed, glad to be scared in a safe way.

Beth smiled and shared a laugh with Janice. Both returned to their seat at the back of the wagon. She felt something on her waist and looked down to see a hand reaching around her. She opened her mouth to scream, but another hand clamped over her mouth and she found herself being drug off the back of the wagon into the darkness. Heavy arms enveloped her. She turned to face her attacker, clawing at the hand covering her mouth.

She found herself looking at a werewolf – all furry and wild looking. The beast smiled at her, and removed his hand only to cover her mouth with his own. He pressed his lips against hers, claiming her mouth as his own. Beth clamped her lips together, too angry to be frightened. She felt his tongue tease her lips, his arms holding her body tightly against his own. She could feel his heat through her clothes, his hardness against her. Her lips parted slightly and his tongue slipped between, barely touching her tongue. Beth found herself molding her body to his, her tongue responding to his, kissing him back.

It was a long, passionate kiss, completely unlike those she had shared with Bob. She could feel the emotion in the kiss, it was a depth like none she'd ever experienced before. He relaxed his grip and looked into her eyes. His eyes were dark and mysterious, but she recognized them immediately. He recognized hers, too, and pulled back.

"Beth?" Beau asked, then swore under his breath. She sank back against the wagon, her legs like spaghetti. He had literally taken her breath away. He stammered, "Oh, jeez, Boss, I'm so sorry. I thought you were Janice. Oh, gosh, I don't believe I just did that."

"It's okay," she said weakly. He shook his head slowly, blinked, and bent down so he could look her in the eye.

"You kissed me back. That kiss was real." Beau said, his voice still thick with emotion.

"I did not. You caught me off guard and scared me," Beth answered, willing herself to be strong and tough. She stood up straight, wiped off her mouth and turned to climb back on the wagon. Thankfully, everyone's attention was still focused on Joe, who was leaping around the wagon, still moaning and groaning. Janice looked at her and smiled, "Did you find Rusty?"

Just then, Rusty leaped up on the tractor, howling like a banshee, making everyone jump and laugh and cheer. Moments later, Beau jumped up on the front of the wagon, also howling and carrying on. Janice clapped gleefully, then moved quickly through the group to jump into Beau's waiting arms.

Beth's smile melted as she watched the two kiss. Beau pulled away, his arm still around Janice. He looked at her, and their gaze locked together. She swallowed hard, willing herself to forget what had just transpired.

CHAPTER SEVENTEEN

Breakfast the morning after the big hay ride was late as usual, and everyone gathered around the table sharing gossip from the night before. The biggest news involved Beau's Aunt Flo. Apparently several people had seen her fire up her big purple rig and pull out, with a man in the cab with her. Rusty reported with a shy smile that it looked like all her stuff had been moved out of the little cabin. Eyebrows raised, and comments were made, but Beau quickly put a stop to the banter, and the tension was palpable.

Beth was the first to excuse herself, then Rusty and Joe headed for the barn. As soon as Katie left to feed the horses, Charlotte flipped two blueberry pancakes onto Beau's plate.

Frank licked his lips and Beau pulled off a little bite of pancake, which Frank took gingerly from his master's hand. Beau poured on the thick maple syrup and dug in hungrily. Charlotte sat down at the end of the table and rested her chin in her hand, watching him eat while the conversation swirled around them. He paused, his fork in mid-air. Syrup hung lazily from the pancake. He looked at his old friend and raised his eyebrows.

"What?"

"What, what?" Charlotte asked, raising her own eyebrows and trying very hard to look innocent. She wasn't succeeding. They had known each other far too long.

"What do you want?"

"What makes you think I want something?" Charlotte countered.

"You never give me extra pancakes without me asking unless you want something," he said flatly. He patted his stomach, "You usually tell me to cut back."

"I guess there's no sense in beatin' around the bush," she said. He looked at her expectantly, and filled his mouth again while waiting for her to go ahead and say what was on her mind. "OK. Beth has tickets to go see the opera in the City tonight. She was supposed to go with her ex-fiance. He cancelled on her, the jerk. She has been on the phone all morning trying to find someone to go with her and nobody will go."

"So? What do you want me to do about it?" he asked, chewing slowly.

"I want you to take her," Charlotte said. Beau choked. Frank woofed.

"You don't mean that," he said. He wiped a tear from his eye with his napkin.

"I most certainly do."

"I don't do opera."

"Listen, that poor girl moved out here to save this ranch. You and I both know that we wouldn't be here if she hadn't come here when her father died. She hasn't had any culture since she came out here, and it would do you good to have a little culture in your life."

Charlotte stood up and started briskly slicing and juicing the oranges that were lined up on the counter. "I'm not asking you to go spend the weekend with her. I'm not asking you to join no damned opera. I'm asking you to do something nice for your boss."

Beau pushed a bite of pancake around on his plate, considering his options. He had no desire to go see some stupid fat lady singing. He always thought it was silly to

Denim & Diamonds

pay money to hear somebody sing when you couldn't even understand what they were singing. And he certainly didn't like the idea of being that close to his boss for an extended period of time. Just the car ride there would be difficult, sitting so close to her, having to carry on a conversation.

On the other hand, Charlotte was right. Beth had given up a lot to take over her father's ranch when the old man died. He watched his friend rub the oranges angrily on the juicer, and contemplated whether or not he should tell her why he had reservations about going on what might be considered a date with his boss.

"Your girlfriend even thinks it would be a good idea for you to take Beth. Beth even went so far as to call Janice, but Janice is tied up with the fair board meeting tonight and can't miss it. It was Janice that called me and suggested that you take Beth."

"Oh," he said. He poked the last of the pancake into his mouth and chewed thoughtfully. One night wouldn't be that bad. Surely he could control himself for one night, and not make a total fool of himself. He tossed back the last drink of Charlotte's specially brewed coffee. "Fine, I'll go talk to her. If she wants me to go with her, I'll go."

Charlotte turned to him and beamed, "Thank you, Beau. She's in the library."

Beau blushed and wiped his mouth with the back of his hand. Frank followed him into the hallway. They stood in the hallway just outside the library for a moment, as Beau tried to gather up his courage to knock on the library door. The door opened and suddenly he and Beth were face to face. She blinked, obviously caught off guard.

"Were you looking for me?" She asked, pink coloring her cheeks.

"Yes. Miss Charlotte was just telling me that you're in a bind tonight. Do you need some help?" Beau asked, his words coming quickly.

"Help?" she asked, tilting her head to the side and looking up at him with wide eyes.

125

"Would you like me to go with you?" he said, slightly impatiently.

She stifled a laugh behind her hand, "You do know I'm going to the opera? Somehow, I just can't picture you at the opera."

"Frankly, neither can I, but that's not the kind of thing you'd want to do by yourself. And you deserve a night out. A nice night out." He closed his eyes, willing himself to quit babbling like some stupid kid. When he opened his eyes, Beth was regarding him seriously.

"Really? You'd do that for me?" she asked softly. She pushed a stray curl out of her eyes and looked up at him with emerald green eyes that took his breath away.

"Sure. I mean, the opera isn't my idea of a great time, but I guess going on a hay ride wasn't your idea of a great time either, right?" he said, then immediately regretted bringing up the hay ride. Neither of them had mentioned the case of mistaken identity, or the kiss they had shared. A smile tugged at the corner of his mouth as he remembered the passion of that kiss. And the way she felt in his arms the night he helped her from her wrecked car. *Stop*!

"That most certainly was not my idea of a good time," Beth said, almost angrily, but not quite. "But I do appreciate your offer to go with me to the opera. You might enjoy it actually. It's Don Giovanni."

"I've never seen him. Is he any good?"

"Don Giovanni is the name of the opera. It's about a ladies' man, and how he gets his comeuppance," she said.

Beau frowned slightly at her description. He wasn't quite sure if his boss was teasing him, or just telling him about the opera. Miss Kitty darted between Beth's legs, stopping to hiss at Frank before running down the hallway with her tail held high.

"So, do you want me to go with you then, or not?" Beau asked, feeling foolish for even offering to go with his boss. She probably had already lined up someone to go

Denim & Diamonds

with her. And even if she didn't, she'd probably prefer to go by herself than with some rough cowboy-type like him.

"You know, this is very nice of you," Beth said. "If you really don't mind going, I would appreciate the company."

"It's settled then," he said, and the two ironed out the specifics. When they finished, she returned to the library and he went to track down Charlotte so she could help him pick out something appropriate to wear to some stupid cultural event that he had no business going to.

Several hours later, Beau found himself in his cramped little bathroom, trying to look at himself in the little mirror over the sink. He carefully trimmed his moustache, using the little electric moustache and beard groomer that the old man had given him for Christmas last year. He put his finger over his moustache and turned his head from side to side, wondering how he'd look without it. Charlotte was right. He'd look like a kid without the moustache. But maybe the Burt Reynolds moustache wasn't in style anymore.

Joe had started wearing a goatee, but Beau just couldn't picture himself doing that. Joe was a couple of years younger than he, and could carry off stuff like that. Beau ran his fingers through his hair and wished he had gone to visit Howie at the barber shop. Charlotte had told him two days ago that he needed a trim, because the hair was starting to poke out over his ears, but he'd been so busy with the mustang, he hadn't had time to get into town. Oh, well, that was the advantage of wearing a cowboy hat. He'd leave the hat on until it was time for the opera and then it'd be dark and Beth wouldn't see what a mess his hair was.

He was wearing his only suit, which was a black western style suit that he had worn when a friend of his got married two summers ago. He hated the tails, but he supposed that was what made the stupid thing dressy. He buttoned his white shirt all the way to the top and slipped his only bolo over his head and adjusted it so it was tight, but not choking him. He picked his black Stetson up off the counter and settled it on his head. Beau smiled at his reflection. Pretty classy, even if he did say so himself!

Back in his room, he examined his dress boots. He had polished them to a high shine before he dressed. They had a few scuffs on them, but not too bad. He pulled them on, then checked his wallet to make sure he had cash. Thank goodness Charlotte had thought about money. If she hadn't had cash to loan him, he would have been up shit creek tonight in the City. He checked his watch. No more stalling. Time to head for the main house and get this show on the road.

The front door opened before he reached the top step. Beth was framed in the doorway, and the sight stopped Beau in mid-stride. Her fiery red curls were pulled up in a loose bun, tendrils curling seductively around her porcelain skin. Her green eyes sparkled as much as the diamond studs in her ears. A single diamond was suspended from a delicate gold chain around her neck, and it drew Beau's eye down to the plunging neckline of Beth's black dress that clung provacatively to her curves. The dress ended a few inches above her knees and Beau smiled appreciatively at her long, lean legs. The high, black heels were the perfect touch.

"Wow," Beau said, shaking his head in disbelief. He'd never imagined that the woman who he found incredibly sexy when dressed in jeans and t-shirts or sweats – and who rarely wore makeup – could look even better.

"Thanks," she said, "You look pretty darned 'wow' yourself."

"Thanks," he said, trying to regain his sense of self-control. He turned slightly and offered his arm. "Shall we?"

Beth stepped forward and tucked her arm in the crook of Beau's arm. They walked to the truck in silence. He opened the passenger door for her and helped her in. He smiled as he realized that her dress was tight enough that she couldn't just hop in like she normally did. After he got

Denim & Diamonds

in and they buckled their seatbelts, he adjusted the heat and flipped on the radio.

After they were on the road, Beth broke the silence by asking Beau about his mustang. He was glad to talk about a subject that was near and dear to his heart – and relatively safe. She had been completely against him getting the mustang, and had been furious with him when he returned to the ranch with the wild stallion. She thought an unpapered horse had no business being on the ranch. It had taken a lot of talking on his part to get her to allow him to keep the stallion at the ranch. Fortunately, she had given in and allowed him to begin gentling the horse. It had proven to be quite a challenge, but a challenge he was enjoying. His voice warmed when he talked about the mustang, and she seemed to be genuinely interested in the progress he was making.

After a while, the two grew quiet and listened to the radio. They chatted intermittently, but mainly just enjoyed the music. After a while, Beau glanced over at Beth and told her she could change channels if she wanted. To his surprise, she tuned in a classic rock station out of the City. When she asked if that was okay with him, he answered with a nod and a smile, a little surprised at her selection, but definitely pleased with her choice of music.

The skyline of the city appeared on the horizon, and Beth perked up visibly at the sight. As they started getting into the city, she pointed out various landmarks and directed Beau on the best way to get to the theater, which was downtown. He cringed when he thought about driving downtown, but Beth was a good navigator. She was so confident of where she was going, and her enthusiasm was catching. It was obvious that she was looking forward to this night out. He had to admit that the lights of the city were beautiful. She guided him into a parking garage that was close to the theater. He felt slightly claustrophobic driving through the garage. It made him a little nervous to have the ceiling so low – his Chevrolet barely fit under the exposed steel beams.

Beth was leaning forward, looking around, obviously anxious to get going. They finally found a parking place where the Silverado fit comfortably, and she immediately reached for the door handle. He reached out and touched her leg, his fingers brushing her skin for the briefest of moments.

"Oh, no, you don't. Wait right here." He jumped out of the truck and jogged around to the passenger side to open her door for her. He took her hand in his as she slid out of the truck. She giggled with excitement and anticipation when she landed, so close to him he could feel her. He again offered his arm, and she tucked her hand in, giving his arm a little hug as she directed them towards the elevator. Beau glanced to the left of the elevator and saw the entrance to the stairwell.

"What do you say we take the stairs?"

Beth gave a little laugh, "Why?"

He blushed and stammered around for a minute, finally admitting, "Elevators make me nervous."

Beth gave a nod and said, "Okay, then. Stairs it is. But you'll have to walk slow. These heels don't go fast down stairs."

He was relieved she didn't make a big deal out of it. He felt bad for her having to go deal with stairs while she had those high heels on – they couldn't be easy to walk in on even ground, much less stairs! But he was awfully thankful he didn't have to get in that little metal box held up by a single cable.

Beth was literally glowing by the time they reached the lobby of the theater. She pulled their tickets out of her beaded black purse that she had been clutching in her hand. When she handed the tickets to the usher, Beau noticed that she had painted her fingernails bright red. He glanced down at his own nails and groaned inwardly when he saw dirt under them. He stuffed his hands in his pockets and hoped she hadn't noticed.

They entered the performance hall and Beau took it all in – the red velvet draped along the walls, the box seats

Denim & Diamonds

to his left and right, the punched tin ceiling and the ornate chandelier. They found their seats and settled into the plush red velvet cushions. There was a white screen hanging above the stage, which reminded Beau of the old screens that his teachers used to put up when they showed a film in class. He pointed to it and asked Beth what the screen was for.

"The supertitles. The performance is in Italian, so they put the English words up on the screen, so it's easy for everyone to follow."

"In Italian? You mean people can really understand what the fat ladies are singing?" Beau asked more sarcastically than he intended. Beth frowned, and kept her gaze directed forward.

"Yes, people can understand the words. And if you'll forget that you don't want to be here, you might enjoy it."

Beau regretted having said anything. He didn't want to be at an opera, but it did give him an opportunity to spend some time with his very attractive boss.

"I'm sorry. I didn't mean it like that. Do you speak Italian?" Beau asked, leaning towards Beth so he could whisper.

"No. I took Spanish in high school and college, but that's it for my foreign language knowledge. But not knowing the language doesn't affect your enjoyment of the performance. Most of the time, I don't even read the words on the screen, I just watch the performers."

Beth seemed willing to forget Beau's rudeness. She flipped through the program, excitedly pointing out various performers that she recognized from previous performances. Several patrons acknowledged her as they made their way to their seats. He glanced at his watch, anxious for the performance to start – so it could get over and they could head back to the ranch. A rather large man scooted down the aisle, taking the seat right next to Beau. The smell was so bad, like rotten eggs, Beau could hardly stand it. He glanced at the man, who was dressed nicely.

131

Elle Robb

Apparently, he hadn't bathed or used deodorant in a while, in spite of his appearance. Beau leaned further towards Beth and discreetly held his finger under his nose. He supposed he could breath through his mouth for the next couple of hours. Or maybe the man would move. There was always hope.

A couple moved into the seats right in front of Beau and Beth. The woman took the seat directly in front of Beth. Beau couldn't believe how big the woman's hair was. He supposed that was high style, but it made it kind of hard for the person behind the hair to see. Beth shifted in her seat, trying to find a way to see around the hair.

He leaned down and whispered, "I'd offer to trade places, but this guy stinks to high heaven."

Beth laughed out loud, but chided him softly, telling him not to be rude. She shifted again in her seat, this time, leaning towards him. He felt her arm against his on the armrest, and her hair brushed his shoulder. He turned slightly towards her and breathed in her scent. It was a warm, sweet smell that reminded him of honey. Then the guy next to him flipped open his program, wafting his strong scent in Beau's direction. He pinched his nose shut and frowned at the man, who was completely oblivious.

The lights dimmed and the curtains opened. Just as Beth had promised, the English translation – which Beau was pretty sure must have been a pretty rough translation, because the performers would sing and sing and sing, and only one sentence would appear on the screen – did appear on the little white screen, which made the opera fairly easy to follow. Beau found himself recognizing some of the words, names in particular. He found himself enjoying the antics of Leparello, and actually laughed out loud a few times. In spite of the fact that he was still holding his nose, he was enjoying himself. Before he knew it, the lights were coming up and it was time for intermission.

Beth led Beau to the lobby, where everyone was milling around. A table filled with wine glasses sat to the side, so he excused himself and got wine for them. When

Denim & Diamonds

he returned to the woman he was beginning to think of as his date, she was talking with a very successful looking man in a well-fitted gray pinstriped suit. With her heels on, she looked the man directly in the eye. The two were leaning towards each other, gesturing and smiling. Beau was surprised to feel a stab of jealousy as he made his way through the crowd, trying not to spill any of the white wine she had requested.

"Thank you, Beau!" Beth said, taking the glass of wine from him. She touched the other man lightly on the arm. "Jackson, this is my ranch foreman, Beau Frakes. And Beau, this is Jackson Steele. He is the executive vice president of FirstBanc."

Beau offered his hand, "Nice to meet you, Mr. Steele."

"Call me Jackson. Nice to meet you, too. I'd better get back to my seat." He leaned towards Beth and whispered loudly, "I'm babysitting one of our clients and you know how demanding those old women can be!"

"All too well, Jackson. Good to see you," Beth said warmly.

"Don't be a stranger, Beth," Jackson winked at Beth, then directed his attention to Beau, "You take good care of your boss and make sure she comes back to us in one piece."

Beau nodded absently. The man's final words echoed in Beau's head. It suddenly occurred to Beau that his boss very well might return to the City once she had served her one year term at the ranch. And why wouldn't she? She was a successful, sophisticated accountant at one of the most prestigious firms in the City. What was there to keep her at the ranch? What if she finished out the year, and then sold the ranch? Not only would Beau stand to lose his job and his home, he was growing quite attached to the lovely lady beside him. It was becoming more and more difficult with each passing day to remember that she was his boss, and he was her employee – nothing more.

Elle Robb

"I know you don't want to be here, but you could wipe that frown off your face so at least everyone else doesn't know. You don't have to be so obvious," Beth whispered fiercely.

Beau tossed back his glass, swallowing his wine in one giant gulp. He took her by the elbow with the intention of walking back towards their seats. Instead, he caught her off guard and she bobbled her wine glass, spilling wine right down her plunging neckline. It was a perfect shot down her cleavage. She glared at him and he withered, just wanting to crawl in a hole. He was all too aware of the stares of those around him. Without a word, Beth handed the glass back to him and turned to go to the ladies' room. He simply stood there, red-faced, smiling awkwardly at the people around him.

Momentarily, she returned. She smiled stiffly and said, "Shall we?"

The two headed for their seats. He started to say something, wanted to say something, but couldn't decide what. The stinky man didn't return for the second act, so Beau leaned away from her, his elbow propped on the armrest and his chin resting in his palm. The lights dimmed and the performance began. He was angry with himself. And he was angry with her for being short with him over what was clearly an unfortunate accident.

When the performance ended and the actors were coming out for their bows, she touched his arm and pointed towards the exit. They scooted along in front of the other patrons, who frowned at the two, and left the theater. Beau turned to Beth to apologize, but just as he began, she dropped suddenly to the sidewalk with a little cry of pain and surprise.

"What the-? Are you okay?" he asked, bending down to take her arm. It was then that he saw the problem. One of her high heels was stuck in a grate in the sidewalk, twisting Beth's ankle at an odd angle. She was squinting up at him, her face pinched. He knelt down on the concrete and gently pulled her foot out of the shoe. He smiled when

Denim & Diamonds

he saw that her toenails were painted the same bright red as her fingernails.

"What the hell are you smiling about?"

"Your red toes. Very cute," Beau answered. She sat back, giving up on keeping her dress clean and nice. He tugged on her shoe, finally pulling it free, but leaving the heel itself in the grate.

"Wonderful, just wonderful," she said, her voice quavering. "I don't think this night could get any worse."

Just then, a flash of lightning lit the sky. They both looked skyward, and a clap of thunder shook the ground. Raindrops started falling. Beau looked down at Beth and saw tears glistening in her eyes. On a whim, he scooped her up in his arms and started for the garage. Her eyes widened, and she started to struggle.

"Just hold still. You can't walk on that ankle. Your dress is ruined. Your shoes are ruined. And we're in the middle of a thunderstorm. Just let me do this," Beau said, his voice tense with anger and frustration. So much for a nice night out. She stopped struggling, and slipped her arm around his neck. After a moment, she leaned her head against his shoulder and sighed.

When they reached the truck, he set her in the truck and leaned down to feel her ankle. It was already swelling. He looked at her, and felt sorry for her when he saw her red, puffy eyes. All he wanted to do was help to give her a nice night out, and nothing had gone right. She sniffled and whispered her thanks. Beau just nodded. He didn't want to admit it, but carrying her up that flight of stairs had winded him. The last thing he wanted to do was make her feel worse. She'd probably think he was saying she was fat.

Instead, he smiled and helped settle her into the seat of the truck. He pulled a heavy coat from the back seat and wadded it up to form a makeshift rest for her foot. Once they were on their way, she told him the best way to get out of the City, which he was thankful for. To be honest, he didn't have the slightest idea where he was or how to get

Elle Robb

out of that spaghetti bowl of highways and roads, especially all those one-way streets that made up the downtown area.

They were finally on the highway headed for the ranch, away from the crowds and traffic of the city. They had driven for quite some time, the windshield wipers making a soothing swish-swish sound and the rain drumming lightly on the cab of the truck. Suddenly, the truck lurched and there was a loud thump-thump-thump. Beau held tightly to the steering wheel as the truck pulled to the left. He slowed and pulled the truck off on the shoulder. Beth sat up straight, her eyes wide.

"Sounds like we got a flat," Beau said, his voice as flat as the tire.

Tonight simply could not get any worse. He didn't know what else could possibly go wrong, and was afraid to consider the possibilities given their run of luck so far. He got out of the truck and, sure enough, the rear tire was completely flat. The reason was clear – a chunk of metal was sticking out of the tire. He sighed and changed the tire as quickly as he could, thankful his hat at least kept the rain from running into his eyes too badly. He banged his knuckles a few times, scuffed his boots up in the gravel and tore his shirt reaching under the truck to get the spare down. He tossed the flat tire in the bed of his truck, and scratched the paint with the metal chunk. He sighed and got back in the truck.

He looked at Beth and, to his surprise and irritation, she started laughing. He looked at her, frizzy red hair going every which way, a wine stain down the front of her dress, and her swollen ankle, and he began to laugh, too. He was sure he was quite a sight himself. They laughed, a good, hearty laugh – the kind shared between good friends. Finally, their laughter died out and they faced each other, both smiling widely.

"I would say it can't get any worse, but I'm afraid to," Beau said.

"Me, too!" Beth joined. "But, you know, it has been memorable."

Denim & Diamonds

"I have to agree with you there. Don't think I'll ever forget my first trip to the opera."

"I'm sorry it turned out like this," Beth said, her tone turning serious.

"Quite all right, Boss. But you owe me!" Beau said, then he started the truck and they were on their way back to the ranch, finally. He turned on the radio, found a soft rock station and the two rode in a companionable silence. Her hand was resting on the seat between them, so he let his hand drop to the seat, too. Their pinkies nearly touched, but not quite. He hesitated to voice the thoughts on his mind, but just couldn't go on without knowing the truth.

"Too bad your fiance couldn't escort you tonight."

She glanced at him, "He's not really my fiance. I broke it off."

"Oh, I'm sorry. Guess the time away has been tough, huh?"

"Not really. It was over before I came to the Domino. I caught him cheating on me."

Beau felt the blood in his cheeks, "I'm sorry. I wouldn't have brought it up if I'd known."

"I know."

He frowned, "But the dinners in town, the phone calls . . . ?"

She shrugged, "Everyone seemed to know he was my fiance, and it was just too embarrassing to explain that our dinners were about business."

"I'm sorry."

"No problem. As long as we're talking," she took a deep breath, "What's the deal with you and Janice? Engaged?"

Beau laughed, "Hardly! Matter of fact, she told me earlier this week that she found herself a job in the City. She's going to be a dancer. She wants the city life, and I want the Domino."

"I know what you mean. There's just something about the ranch."

Elle Robb

They grew quiet, each caught up in their own thoughts. There was plenty to think about. Beau caught Beth staring out the window and asked her if she was bored.

"No, I was just looking for constellations. The clouds are clearing and there are stars everywhere. When I was a little girl, my father took me to the planetarium and thought it was one of the neatest things I'd ever seen. I've been fascinated with the stars ever since." Beth gave a self-conscious laugh, "I know this is silly, but it sort of makes me feel like everything is possible. Like my problems are so little, and there is so much out there . . ."

"I understand. I like to look at the stars, too. Always thought astronauts had the coolest job."

"Absolutely!" Beth turned slightly in her seat to face Beau, "Would you go if you had the chance?"

"What? To the stars?" he asked, glancing over at her. She was absolutely gorgeous, bathed in the pale light of the dashboard.

"To the moon. To space. Whatever."

"I'd probably go. Just to get away. Sometimes things get too complicated down here." He shrugged and shook his head. "It'd be incredible. Like the pictures of the earth taken from the moon. Those are pretty neat."

The two continued to talk, and Beth pointed out a few constellations in the night sky until they turned into the ranch. In spite of her protests, he insisted on carrying her to the front door of the main house. She promised to go see the doc the next day, and gave him a quick peck on the cheek before shutting the door. Beau thought it was a perfect ending to a wonderful evening.

Denim & Diamonds

CHAPTER EIGHTEEN

Beth wiped her mouth and looked around the big table at the people she was beginning to think of as family. This was the first Thanksgiving she had spent away from her mother and, quite frankly, she didn't miss it. She had called her mother before dinner to wish her a Happy Thanksgiving and to catch up, but she felt perfectly at home here at the ranch. She was in the place of honor at the head of the table, and Beau was sitting opposite her. She had asked if Janice would be joining them, but Beau had mumbled something about other plans.

To her right sat Joe and Rusty, who apparently didn't have any family nearby, and across from the two ranch hands were Charlotte and Katie. Katie's parents had gone to the Caribbean for the long weekend, so she was spending the holiday at the ranch, which was where she spent most of her time anyway.

Everyone's plates were piled with seconds, and they had barely made a dent in the feast that Charlotte had prepared. She had been working on this meal all week long, and she practically beamed every time someone asked for a dish to be passed. The huge turkey in the center of the table still had a little meat left on it, but not much. Beth couldn't recall ever seeing so much food prepared for a single meal in her entire life.

Elle Robb

After everyone had finished the main course, Beth and Katie cleared away the dishes and prepared containers of leftovers for each of the guests to take with them. Charlotte made sure they gave generous portions of leftovers for the boys to take back to their house. Beth sat back down at a table now laden with pies of every kind imaginable. She was full, but her mouth watered when she saw the apple pies and pumpkin pies. Like the others, she had a difficult time deciding which pie to have. She decided on the pumpkin, and found it absolutely incredible.

Finally, everyone's plates were clean and they were all sitting back in their chairs, laughing and talking. Beth's family dinners had always been formal affairs, where the conversation was polite and the attire was dressy. She had balked at first, but Charlotte had convinced her that sweats were perfectly acceptable – and preferable – at Thanksgiving dinner. At this point, Beth was glad she'd gone with the elastic waist!

Rusty glanced at his watch and announced it was time for the football game to start. The guys headed for the living room and soon they could be heard cheering and booing. Beth stayed in the kitchen with Katie and Charlotte, cleaning up. This had always been the job of the hired help while she was living at home with her mother, but Beth actually enjoyed it. It was satisfying to clean up after a good meal – and the women laughed and joked and talked. When they were finished, they moved into the living room and the boys caught them up on the scores, who was winning and who they wanted to win, and they all cheered and jeered. She had never been a football fan, but the enthusiasm of the others was contagious.

After a while, she noticed that Charlotte and Katie had disappeared. She turned to look for them just as they appeared in the doorway. Katie was carrying her boombox and a large thermos, and Charlotte was carrying a chainsaw. Joe followed Beth's gaze and let out a whoop. Rusty saw Charlotte about the same time and let out a holler of his own. Before Beth knew what was happening,

Denim & Diamonds

they were piled on the wagon and Beau was driving the tractor, heading for the woods. Katie fired up her boom box and Christmas music filled the air. Everyone sang along. Beth found herself blushing as she stumbled through the words to the Twelve Days of Christmas. Charlotte caught her eye and smiled. Rusty looked at her and gave her the thumbs up sign.

The weather was perfect for their task. The sky was gray, and looked as though it could snow. The air was brisk and she was glad she had chosen her fleece jacket, so she could pull the collar up around her ears and tuck her hands into the deep pockets.

When they reached the woods, they started pointing out trees that appeared to be good Christmas tree prospects. The first tree Katie pointed out was perfectly proportioned, but Charlotte vetoed it because it would be too tall to fit in the living room. Rusty found a tree that was the right height, but it was awfully wide. Then Beth spotted a tree that was beautiful – it was just like she always imagined. The tree stood by itself, and a ray of sunlight broke through the clouds and shone directly on the full evergreen. Joe hopped off and volunteered to do the cutting. There was good natured teasing as Beau suggested that he didn't know if Joe could be trusted with a chainsaw, and there were several references made to the possibility of missing limbs and appendages.

Back at the ranch, Joe and Rusty put the tree in the stand, carefully adjusting the tree so that it would stand up straight. Charlotte served as their eyes and directed them left and right, front and back, until satisfied the tree was as straight as it could be. Miss Kitty took a great interest in the goings on and, the first chance she had, she jumped from her perch on the back of the sofa and climbed the tree. It took Beth several minutes to coax the calico out of the tree so that the lights could be strung and they could proceed with putting the ornaments on the tree.

There was lots of laughter and talking as the ornaments were pulled from the green and red storage containers. Each ornament seemed to have a story, and Beth was impressed with the history that this little group shared. Several references were made to her father, and Beth couldn't help but feel a little left out and a bit bitter that these people had happier memories of her father than she did. And it made her wish she had made more of an effort while her father had been alive. She found herself offering up a prayer of thanks for his final wishes sending her here.

"Look, everybody! It's snowing!" Katie shouted, pointing out the big picture window. Sure enough, big, fluffy flakes were floating down and were already sticking to the glass. Everyone cheered and predictions were made about how much snow would stick.

Charlotte opened the entertainment armoire and tuned the radio to the local station, which was playing Christmas music. Beth was placing blue and silver glass ball ornaments on the tree when "Jingle Bells" came to an end and a newsbreak replaced the music. Nobody paid much attention until the weather came on.

"And now for the Moscow area forecast – be prepared to bundle up and hibernate. This snow storm has blown up out of nowhere. The two inches that we were predicting has been upgraded. The weather center is now predicting twelve to fourteen inches. Of course, the biggest problem is the rain that we had last night. Dropping temperatures are creating ice, and ice can be a real problem. The highway patrol is suggesting that you only get out on the roads if absolutely necessary. And now for an update on sports-"

"Woo-hoo!" Katie shouted, skipping around the room, "We're gonna be snowed in!"

Beth smiled at the display of youthful exuberance. At least it was a long holiday weekend and there wasn't really a need to be out on the roads. She glanced around and decided if she was going to be snowed in, this was a good place to be.

Denim & Diamonds

After the tree was decorated, everyone wandered into the kitchen and started heating up leftovers. A few decided that cold turkey was just fine, and Joe and Rusty went straight for the pie. Charlotte had just chased everyone out of the kitchen so she could get things cleaned up when the lights flickered. They flickered again, and then the house stayed dark. Beth shivered at the thought of being without electricity.

The idea didn't seem to bother Beau though, who took control. He sent the men out to get firewood, and sent Katie to the linen closet to get a few extra blankets. He got the fire going, and everyone settled down to enjoy the crack and pop and warmth of the fire. The wind howled outside, sounding cold. The glow of the fire provided a gentle light in the room.

After a few minutes of silence, they started trading stories about other blackouts. Beth shivered when Charlotte related the story of the ice storm of '98, when they were stuck at the ranch without power for three days. Beau added that the hardest part of being without power on the ranch was watering the livestock, and reminded Joe and Rusty that they'd have to help him break water on the tanks in the morning if the power hadn't been restored. Beth asked about an emergency generator, but Charlotte laughed.

"Your father would have never allowed us to have an emergency generator. He thought that was part of the fun of being way out here. Said it reminded him of how it must have been in the old days," Beau explained.

At Katie's urging, the group started playing charades. Beth couldn't recall ever having actually played charades before. When she got together with friends in the City, there always seemed to be more structure to it. The games they played came in boxes, and often involved a DVD player.

The wind continued to howl outside, and Beau added wood to the fire. It was starting to get late, and one by one, the group started pulling blankets around

Elle Robb

themselves. Beth found herself on one end of the sofa, with Beau sitting next to her. Charlotte asked Katie to go to the kitchen with her to get the makings for spiced cider. Rusty produced a long wrought iron tool and held the black tea kettle over the fire until the water was heated. Charlotte and Katie prepared the mugs of hot cider and distributed them. Beth cupped the mug in her hands, enjoying the warmth and the spicy scent of the cider. She stirred the cider with the cinnamon stick that Katie had handed her. She closed her eyes and drank, feeling warm and safe and comfortable.

Sunlight in her eyes awoke Beth the next morning. It took her a moment to realize where she was. She was leaning against the arm of the sofa, and Beau was leaning against her. They were covered with a heavy blanket that was tucked around them. Rusty and Joe were sprawled on the other side of the couch, also sharing a blanket. Katie was curled up in the corner, her mouth wide open, with Frank laying against her. Charlotte was leaned back in her recliner, her sock feet sticking out from underneath her blanket. Beth's leg was asleep, so she tried to shift it carefully, but Beau stretched and blinked. He looked at her, his eyelids still heavy with sleep. He sat up and Beth immediately missed the warmth of his body. It was awfully cold, and the fire was nothing but a few glowing coals.

Beau padded across the room in his sock feet, shivering in the chilly morning air. He quickly got the fire roaring again, and Beth was thankful for the warmth it put out. She snuggled deeper in the blanket, wondering how much longer it would be before the power came on.

Charlotte opened her eyes and stretched. She turned to Beth, seeming to read her mind, "It shouldn't be much longer. I'm sure they'll get to us sometime today."

"I hope so," Katie said from the corner, pulling the blanket closer around her.

Joe and Rusty stretched and yawned, then pulled their boots on. It took Beth a moment to realize what they were doing – taking care of the stock. She reached for her own boots.

Denim & Diamonds

"You don't have to go. We got it." Beau said, dropping onto the sofa and pulling his boots on.

"They're mine, too. The more people helping, the faster it'll get done, right?" Beth countered. She was well aware of the fact that the weather was a serious danger to the horses. And she could not afford to lose any of the horses. The yearlings were to be sold in the spring, and the two year olds had already been spoken for. Deposits had been made on them and, quite frankly, had already been spent on feed and fencing. The ranch – and Beth was well aware that meant her – could not afford to lose any animals.

"If you're going out with us, you'd better change into some warm clothes. Go put some long johns on, and coveralls would be good, too," Beau ordered.

"What about that mountain lion? Should we take a gun?" Beth asked nervously.

"Don't need to worry about any mountain lions. That threat is gone, now." Beau answered.

Beth and Charlotte looked at each other with raised eyebrows, but decided to let the odd comment pass.

The bitter cold hit hard, burning her lungs with every breath. She pulled the stocking cap down further over her ears and followed in Beau's tracks. It had finally stopped snowing, but it was well over her boots. The wind was blowing straight out of the north, and large drifts had formed in the driveway and at the front of the barn. Beau's mustang whinnied from his run. His form gradually took shape in the blowing snow. Beau headed for the stallion, and Beth went right, towards the broodmares' stalls. The horses were huddled in the innermost parts of their stalls, all shivering. The snow had blown in from the north, piling snow inside. Joe handed Beth a hammer and told her to break the ice, then use the claw to pull the chunks out so the horses could drink. Beth made her way down the aisle, opening the doors and slipping into each stall so she could do as she had been told. The mares drank eagerly as soon as she had broken the ice. Katie followed her, quickly scooping the old straw out into the aisle. By the time they

145

got to last stall, Beth could barely make her fingers grip the hammer. Katie was shivering badly.

They made their way back down the aisle and climbed the ladder to the hayloft. Beth tossed hay down into the corner racks and Katie tossed down bales of straw. The two worked quickly side by side, without talking, intent on their tasks. Once finished with the hay and straw, they hurried down the ladder. Beth headed for the feed room and started filling the feed bunks, while Katie used the pitchfork to spread the warm straw in the stalls. By the time they finished, Katie was shivering uncontrollably. Beth hollered over to Beau, who said he had the boys (as he referred to his stallion, Digger and Dingo) under control. He yelled over the blowing wind for Beth to get Katie up to the house so she could warm up, but asked Beth if she'd go with him to check on the yearlings in the east pasture. Rusty and Joe had gone out on the four-wheelers to the west pasture to check on the two year olds. They had a three-sided shelter there that served as pretty good protection for them, and Beau was confident they would be huddled up together keeping warm. Beau was a little worried that the yearlings, though, and wanted to check on them himself.

After Beth made sure Katie made it to the house okay, she met Beau in the driveway. She got on the four-wheeler behind him, holding on tight and tucking her face into his back to protect herself from the wind. The going was slow, even though the ATV had snow tires on it and was four-wheel drive. The trek to the east pasture seemed to take forever, but Beth realized that it was much easier going on the ATV than it would have been trying to go by foot, even though the blowing wind was nearly unbearable. The tires slipped in the heavy snow and they fishtailed several times, but they continued to make forward progress.

At the gate to the east pasture, Beau brought the ATV to a stop. The snow was up to the second rung of the gate, so it would be impossible to open the gate to take the vehicle through. Beau and Beth swung off the ATV and

Denim & Diamonds

climbed the gate. None of the yearlings were in sight. As before, Beth walked directly behind Beau, following in his footsteps, as they made their way towards the shelter she referred to as the "horsey house".

She was glad he seemed to have a good sense of direction – she was disoriented in the blinding snow, and wasn't entirely sure which way they should go. Just as she was about to ask Beau if he was sure about their path, the shape of the shelter appeared in the blowing snow. The wind was at their backs, thankfully, pushing them towards the shelter. The snow was heavy, pulling at their boots with every step. It was so cold and so wet, and was packing down into the sides of Beth's boots. Finally, they reached the shelter. They could hear animals moving inside, and Beth was relieved to round the corner and see the six yearlings standing together, head to tail. They turned to look at the humans that had disturbed them, and nickered softly. Their eyelashes looked like icicles. They were soaked to the bone, and were shivering violently. The bay's tail was weighted down with a heavy snowball that had formed as he walked through the snow. Their water tank was nearly frozen solid.

Beau instructed Beth to climb up into the little loft and toss down straw and hay. He pulled a t-post from the corner of the shelter and used it to bust up the ice in the tank. He pulled chunks of ice out with his hands and threw them outside the shelter. Beth saw him clapping his hands together and slapping his legs, trying to keep the blood circulating. His gloves appeared to be frozen, and they cracked when he clapped them together.

The yearlings eagerly munched on the fresh hay that Beth had tossed down. She skipped the last couple of rungs coming down the ladder and jumped into the thick straw. Quickly, she pulled the flakes of straw apart and spread it around the shelter. Beau continued to work on the water tank, and instructed her to use handfuls of straw to dry the horses.

Both Beau and Beth were numb by the time they finished. They started the long walk back to the ATV, and Beth was glad to see that the wind was dying down somewhat. Her toes were past hurting, and were completely numb, causing her to stumble a bit as she walked. She saw Beau doing the same thing, and knew they'd better get back to the ranch soon so they could get warmed up. The ride back to the warmth of the fire seemed to take forever, but the feeling of camaraderie between them was comforting.

Once inside the main cabin, they quickly changed into clean, dry clothes and huddled in front of the fire to warm up. Her fingers and toes burned as the blood began to flow freely again, and she winced at the pain. Just as she was starting to feel her fingers again, the lights flickered on and the furnace roared to life. She closed her eyes and offered up a silent prayer of thanks, both for the return of electricity and the fact that she had such a wonderful crew of people to help her keep the Domino running no matter what. She was all too aware of the fact that she needed their help to make the ranch profitable – this definitely wasn't a job for a loner. And she only had a few short months left before her father's attorney would make the final determination as to whether or not she would be able to collect on her father's bequest.

Denim & Diamonds

CHAPTER NINETEEN

Beth woke up with a start. She rubbed her neck, irritated with herself for having fallen asleep. The financial books containing the ranch records were spread out across her father's desk, and the legal pad to her right contained lots of her scribbles and notes. She still gripped the mechanical pencil in her right hand. It was a time of reckoning, and she was scared to death.

It occurred to her that a year ago, she wouldn't have thought this would be such a big deal. When her father's Will had been read, she had thought it would do her good to get out of the City for a while, to get over Bob's betrayal. The million dollars would have been a nice extra, but she led a fairly comfortable life as it was, and money just wasn't that important to her, so it just hadn't seemed like a big deal at the time. A bit of a challenge, yes, but not a do or die situation. Now, a year later, it was.

She had come to care for the people here at the Domino Ranch as family, not merely as employees. They had supported and cared for her, and taught her more in the past year than she ever could have imagined. And now it was down to the wire, and no matter how many times she ran the figures, she couldn't show a profit for the past year.

"Breakfast is ready!" Charlotte called from the kitchen.

Elle Robb

Beth rubbed her eyes and rolled her head back and forth, trying to work the kinks out. Dejected, she headed for the kitchen, and what would most likely be her last breakfast as the owner of the ranch. Bright sunlight was streaming through the window over the sink, seeming to mock her with its brightness. It was going to be a beautiful spring day. Under the terms of her father's will, if she was unable to show that she could run the ranch at a profit, it was to be sold at public or private auction, at her father's lawyer's discretion.

She poked around at her scrambled eggs, unable to summon any appetite. Charlotte busied herself at the counter, where she was whipping up a batch of peanut butter cookies. Beth was aware of the glances Charlotte was sneaking over her shoulder, but pretended not to notice. She flinched when she heard the crunch of gravel, followed by Frank barking on the front porch, and then a solid knock at the door.

She stood up slowly and answered the door herself. She greeted Mr. Cooper, and they exchanged pleasantries. He smiled at her, almost apologetically, and cleared his throat.

"Well, you know why I'm here. It's time for the year-end evaluation of the Domino Ranch, to finally carry out your father's wishes," he said solemnly. His black suit seemed to mirror his demeanor.

"Before we get down to the nuts and bolts of it, why don't I show you around the ranch?" Beth said, putting on a brave face. She was worried about what would happen to the people who called the Domino home. In spite of the fact that she had failed, she was still proud of the ranch. She felt like she had accomplished so much in the past year and her heart was breaking at the thought of losing all she had worked so hard for.

The attorney considered the offer for a moment, seemed about to decline, then nodded and said, "You know, that would be nice. Your father thought a lot of this place, and I haven't been here since he passed away."

Denim & Diamonds

As Beth and Mr. Cooper walked towards the barn, she pointed out the things that she liked best about the ranch, and related some of the things that she had learned during the past year. The lawyer listened politely, then shared a personal story about visiting the ranch, and the trail ride that her father had taken him on, which happened to be his only experience with riding horses. When he described the horse he had ridden, Beth immediately realized that he had ridden Dingo. She smiled and told him about her first experience with riding on the ranch, also on Dingo. He laughed out loud when she told how she had gotten sick on her first ride.

Beth was proud of the ranch, and was eager to point out the changes that had evolved over the past year. Her father had loved the ranch, but she had added her own special touches to the place over the past year. She showed Mr. Cooper the freshly painted red barn trimmed in white, the well-organized office, the tack room that smelled of saddle soap, and the feed room that now featured convenient, rodent-proof containers that had been her idea. Each stall now had a card holder next to the bronze nameplate that held a large index card containing information about feed, worming and breeding. The barn smelled of fresh hay and straw, and the aisle had been neatly raked, thanks to the efforts of Katie.

Beth spoke to each horse by name, and reached through the stall door to pet each eager nose. When they reached the arena, they stopped to watch Beau working a two-year old on the lunge line. The sorrel was flashy, with a wide blaze down his face and white stockings. He was muscular, and his hindquarters were particularly well developed. The horse's ears swiveled constantly, listening to Beau's instructions. Beau acknowledged the visitors with a brief nod, but continued to concentrate on the horse.

When they left the arena and walked down the other aisle, Beth noticed a distinct frown on the older man's face when they reached the mustang's stall. The red horse stood tall, his head held high. He snorted and pawed the floor of

151

his stall when they approached the door. She repeated what Beau had told her about the mustang's strength, stamina and agility, which would make him an asset to the ranch's cutting horse breeding program. Mr. Cooper gave a brief shake of his head.

"With all due respect, Beth, I disagree. Your father chose each and every breeding animal with great care. You have his pedigree books – he studied them the way an artist studies the great Impressionists. He always said the most important part of the breeding program is the stallion. The stallion is the hub of the operation – without a top quality stud, you don't have a top drawer program."

She listened silently, her head down. She knew he was right. She also remembered all too clearly the argument she had with Beau regarding how to replace her father's stallion when he had died last summer, furious she had been when he defied her and bought the wild stallion, and how impressed she had been with the mustang as his training progressed. She bit her tongue, though – it just didn't matter anymore.

As they left the barn, Beth turned the conversation to the cattle, and invited the attorney to join her for a quick ride on the Gator which was parked just outside the barn. It gleamed in the bright sunlight, and Beth smiled as she realized that Katie must have waxed the vehicle. Beth took the driver's seat and the attorney sat stiffly beside her, his briefcase clutched tightly on his lap. The wooden fencing along the front of the ranch and the driveway had just been painted white, and gleamed in the early summer sunlight. The grass was green and fresh flowers bloomed along the graveled paths, thanks to Charlotte's green thumb. They passed large pastures where the polled Herefords were grazing peacefully.

Beth stopped in front of the pasture where the bull was kept. He was grazing close to the fence, so Beth stopped and hopped out. Mr. Cooper watched in amazement as the bull approached Beth and let her reach over the fence and scratch his wooly face. She couldn't

Denim & Diamonds

help but remember what she was like when she had walked into his office a year ago – that girl was actually petting a 1,500 pound bull!

When they reached the pasture where the broodmares and their foals were kept, Beth felt like she was going to burst with pride. The mares continued to graze as the ATV approached, but the foals watched curiously, their broomstick tails flipping back and forth. A couple came forward, and a couple stood behind their mothers, peeking out from behind them to watch the strangers approach. Mr. Cooper had to admit they were fine looking animals.

After Beth had given the attorney the tour, she grudgingly turned the Gator back towards the main house. The two were silent, both deep in their own thoughts. Back at the house, Beth led the older man to her father's library, her expression solemn. Charlotte met them at the door, wiping her hands anxiously on her apron.

"Want me to bring in tea?" Charlotte asked, concern lining her face.

"No," Beth took the seat behind her father's desk, where she waited for the gavel to fall. Mr. Cooper took a seat in one of the leather chairs facing the desk and placed his briefcase on the desk. He flipped it open, removed a sheaf of papers and scooted the briefcase to the side. She swallowed hard, sat up straight and folded her hands in front of her to keep them from shaking.

"I see you've been running the numbers yourself, Beth," he said, gesturing to the piles of papers littering the big desk.

"Yes, and I can't say that I am pleased with the result," she said, feeling dejected and forlorn.

"Nor am I. I've gone over your books several times, trying to make this work. Your father really wanted you to succeed, but you just aren't managing the ranch well. This is a business, and you aren't running it like a business," he said gently. The words still stung, though, and she winced visibly.

153

Elle Robb

"I don't know how binding my father's Will is, but if there is any way--"

"I'm afraid it's ironclad," the attorney interrupted. "Your father's wishes were very deliberate and precise. With all due respect, Beth, I am surprised that you failed. What makes my job very difficult is that you were close. You nearly pulled it off, but you made too many mistakes. You allowed the purchase of a stallion that held no value whatsoever, you made personal loans to employees without collecting, you gave bonuses at Christmas when the ranch didn't have the money to spare. That's just the tip of the iceberg – the parties you threw, the new fence you put up, buying the highest quality feed. The list goes on and on, I'm afraid."

Every word was like a knife in Beth's chest. It physically hurt to have him point out her multitude of failures. Then came the final twist.

"I'm afraid the ranch will be sold, because the books clearly do not show a profit. Pursuant to the terms of your father's Will, you and the staff will have ten days to remove yourself and your possessions from the property. The livestock will be taken to the sale barn and sold to the highest bidder."

She felt lightheaded, and fought to keep the tears from spilling over. Her head was spinning, and she suddenly thought about Dingo. Who would take care of him? What would happen to him? What would Charlotte do? And worst of all – would Beau ever forgive her? Would she ever see him again?

"Excuse me, Boss, but I need to make a payment." Beth's head swiveled to the left. Rusty was standing in the doorway, his worn hat clenched in his hands. He stepped forward and handed her a fistful of cash, "You loaned me money last summer to get a new transmission for my pickup. I'm payin' you back, with interest, just like I promised. Sorry it took me so long. Ma'am."

Beth took the money, dumbfounded. She recalled giving him the money for the repair, but they hadn't

154

Denim & Diamonds

discussed the terms of repayment. She hadn't expected him to pay it back. He excused himself, and backed out of the room, nodding as he went. She and Mr. Cooper were left staring at each other. Before they could speak, Joe appeared at the door.

"Hey, Boss, I need to make a payment, too," Joe said. He pulled nervously at his goatee, then placed a handful of wadded bills on the desk in front of Beth. "That's my payment for the money you loaned me in April when I didn't have enough money to pay my taxes. Thanks, again."

As soon as Joe left the room, Katie walked in. She was grinning from ear to ear, and she was holding a check. With a flourish, she handed the check to an open-mouthed Beth, and said, "My dad told me to give this to you. He says he owes you rent for all the nights you let me spend the night here, and board, too, for all the food I eat here. He says I live here more than I live at home."

Katie gave a little curtsey and winked, "And he's right!"

The girl turned to leave, meeting Charlotte on her way out. Beth bit her lower lip and nodded a greeting to Charlotte, noting the cash rolled up in the housekeeper's plump hand.

"Sorry to interrupt again. I'm sorry I didn't have this to you sooner. I've been collecting UPC symbols and sending off for rebates, plus I've been keeping track of the money I've saved in coupons. Here's what I saved this year. It needs to be deposited in the ranch operating account, but I thought I'd let you do it," Charlotte explained, adding her cash to the growing pile of money sitting in the center of the desktop.

When Charlotte left the room, Mr. Cooper cleared his throat and said, "This is an interesting development, but I don't know if this is going to be enough—"

Numbers were swirling in Beth's head, and the accountant in her came to life. Beth's voice cracked when she spoke, "But you said I was close. I *know* how close I

155

am. We made an excellent profit on the cattle this year, and we made top dollar on the two year olds we sold for the rodeo circuit. I made mistakes, I know, but if my figures are right, all I need is about $7,000 in order to show a profit."

Mr. Cooper pulled a small notebook from his breast pocket. His countenance was serious, and he contemplated the figures before nodding slowly, "The books show a deficit of just slightly less than $6,000."

Beth said up straight in her father's chair and took a deep breath. "Let's see what we have then."

Her slender fingers hovered over the keys of her father's old desktop calculator, and Mr. Cooper pulled a small handheld calculator from his briefcase. Beth closed her eyes and sent up a silent prayer. She counted the cash and then counted it again. "I get $3,820 in cash."

She handed the bills to the attorney and watched as he counted twice.

"I get the same," he said, laying the money in a neat stack on the desk. "How much is the check for?"

Beth picked up Katie's check, "It's written for $1,200."

Beth sighed and her shoulders slumped considerably. She didn't need a calculator to tell her that she was still short. She bit her lower lip and tears stung her eyes. It was over.

"I'm sorry, Beth," Mr. Cooper said softly.

"So am I, Mr. Cooper, so am I," she whispered and closed her eyes, fighting the tears. She heard footsteps in the hallway and the door creaked as it swung open. She opened her eyes and saw Beau standing in the doorway, he was tall and dark and handsome, but right now, Beth needed a knight in shining armor, not a cowboy. She shook her head at him and said, "It's over. I didn't make it."

"Don't sell yourself short, Boss," Beau said, his expression serious. In two quick strides, he was standing beside the desk, laying his own check on the table. "This is to pay you back for the mustang. When I bought him with

Denim & Diamonds

ranch funds, I promised you I would pay you back. Well, I'm paying you back."

Beth's eyes opened wide and she quickly picked the check up. It was made out to Domino Ranch, in the amount of $2,000. A smile spread across her face, and her green eyes danced with delight. "It's enough! This is it! It's enough!"

On impulse, Beth jumped to her feet and threw her arms around Beau's neck, planting a kiss on his lips. He blinked in surprise, then kissed her back. Together, they turned to the attorney, their arms around each other's waists. She spoke first, "It is enough, Mr. Cooper, isn't it?"

The attorney didn't speak immediately. He smiled an enigmatic smile and pushed some papers aside so he could set his briefcase on the desk. Beth and Beau exchanged worried glances, and Beth felt like her heart was in her throat. Her father's grandfather clock ticked loudly, and blood rushed in her ears. She watched as Mr. Cooper produced an ivory colored, official looking envelope, and a large, business-style checkbook. With a flourish, he produced a fountain pen from his breast pocket and wrote out a check. His expression was solemn. Beth was holding her breath, and felt Beau's grip tighten on her waist. Finally, the attorney carefully pulled the check from the checkbook and stood up.

"It is with great pleasure, Elizabeth Pickard, that I present you with the deed to the ranch." The attorney handed her the official looking envelope, "In that envelope you will also find the gift affidavit which your father executed before his death. It gives all the personal property, equipment and livestock to you. It was his wish that I hold that until you had lived on the ranch for a year."

"Thank you," she whispered as she held the envelope to her chest.

"And here is your check for one million dollars, as promised," Mr. Cooper handed her the check, bowing slightly as he did so, "It is my pleasure to present this to you. Congratulations on a job well done."

Tears streamed down Beth's cheeks and suddenly her legs felt like they were about to give out. There was a shout from the hallway, the door flung open and people spilled into the library – Beth felt herself being hugged and slapped on the back – Charlotte had tears streaming down her face, Katie was dancing around the room, and Joe and Rusty were whooping and hollering and giving high fives all around. Frank was jumping excitedly, barking at everyone.

Beth called for everyone's attention. It took nearly a minute for the small group to quiet down enough for her to speak. And when she did, her voice cracked with emotion, "I just want to say thank you. You are the most wonderful group of friends anyone could ever hope for. You pulled together, and helped me when you didn't have to. Over the past year, you have become my closest friends. More than that, you became my family when I didn't have a family." Beth held her check high and continued, "And the bonuses this year are going to be *awesome!*"

The little group erupted in laughter and loud cheers. It was pure chaos, until the attorney rapped his knuckles loudly against the desk.

"There is one more piece of business to take care of, and then I will leave you all to celebrate," he said, leaning over the desk to write out another check. Beth looked at Beau, but he just shrugged and arched his eyebrows.

"Beauregard Frakes, it is with great pleasure that I carry out my last duty as Mr. Pickard's personal representative and trustee," Mr. Cooper said, finally smiling, "It was Mr. Pickard's wish to leave you, his dear and loyal friend, a cash bequest of one million dollars."

Beau's jaw went slack, and he looked as though he could be pushed over with a touch. He took the offered check and stared at it. Then he spoke, his voice barely a whisper, "But why? I had no idea. Why now?"

"It was Mr. Pickard's wish that you be rewarded if you showed your loyalty to the ranch by remaining here to help his daughter succeed. He wanted you to help her on

Denim & Diamonds

your own, and he didn't want there to ever be any doubt in anyone's mind, especially his daughter's, that you might have been motivated by greed."

Beau lifted his eyes and looked at each person in the room, one by one, then his gaze settled on Beth and he finally smiled, happiness washing over his features. It was as if the chains that had bound him had fallen free. Without taking his eyes off her, he said, "Thank you, Mr. Cooper. You have no idea what this means to me."

"Good luck to you all. It has been a pleasure—" Mr. Cooper said, snapping his briefcase closed.

Beau took Beth's hands in his. Beth looked up at him, her emerald green eyes still glistening with unshed tears. A hush fell over the room and all eyes focused on the cowboy and the heiress. Her head was spinning, and she barely heard Beau speak to her.

"Elizabeth Pickard, I'm not one for fancy words, but I have loved you since the moment I pulled you from your wrecked car. I loved you when you got sick on me and then passed out in my arms. I loved you when you helped me with the horses even in the middle of a blizzard. I love you more than words can say. I know I'm just an uncultured cowboy, but would you do me the honor of having dinner with me tonight, to celebrate?"

A single tear fell down Beth's cheek and she nodded, "Yes, oh, yes! I love you, too!"

Joe let out a whoop, and the room quickly turned to a loud celebration, with hugs all around. Even Mr. Cooper got in on the celebration, and gave Beth a hug and a peck on the cheek. Charlotte slipped out of the room and returned moments later with a bottle of champagne and several crystal flutes. The attorney did the honors, pulling the cork with a loud pop, and filling the flutes.

"The old man always said this should be kept for a special occasion. I think this is pretty special," Charlotte said, giving Beau a peck on the cheek and then hugging Beth. Everyone raised their glasses in a toast. Frank woofed his approval, his feathery tail wagging furiously.

Elle Robb

Beau kept hold of Beth's hand the whole time, his dark eyes sparkling. She looked up at him and could scarcely believe this was real. It was like a dream come true, and she didn't ever want to let go of him.

He leaned down and whispered to her, his breath tickling her ear, "You don't have a boyfriend, do you?"

She looked up into his shining eyes and laughed, "No -- I'm all yours, Beau."

ABOUT THE AUTHOR

Elle makes her home in central Missouri, where she lives with her husband and daughter. They share their home with 2 very spoiled Miniature Schnauzers, a barn kitty that rarely sleeps in the barn, and several Miniature Horses.

For more information, a calendar of upcoming events, and contest information, visit her website at www.ellerobb.com.

Elle Robb